Mostly Invisible

Also by Mario Milosevic

Novels
Claypot Dreamstance • *The Coma Monologues* • *The Doctor and the Clown*
Kyle's War • *The Last Giant* • *Splitting* • *Terrastina and Mazolli*

Collections
Entangled Realities (with Kim Antieau)
Labor Days • *Miniatures*
20 Strange Tales of Crime and Mystery

Poetry
Animal Life
Fantasy Life
Love Life

Mostly Invisible

Mario Milosevic

Green Snake
PUBLISHING

Mostly Invisible
by Mario Milosevic

ISBN: 978-1-949644-58-6

Cover image: © Annie Spratt | Unsplash

Published by Green Snake Publishing
www.greensnakepublishing.com

Contents

Beginnings: above the surface

The stowaway was too handsome to execute • Stories, like icebergs, keep much of themselves hidden from view • Beginnings are easy • Before the end of the show, Mark knew he was going to applaud • I have it on the highest authority that fairies were not always so shy as they are now and in the old days you would see them every-where: ambling down sidewalks, taking bites out of fruit at the market, and often in living rooms, where they would put their feet up on the remote and watch whatever was on TV • Kay lived the life we all wanted but couldn't have • It has always bothered me that mothers-in-law have such a bad reputation in folk-tales • When I woke up, all the animals could talk and I understood them, every one of them • You think *your* job is hard, try taking care of a giant • A sleep-soaked room will always remind Missy of the home she never had • Ward took over after all the adults died because he was the oldest and he said he knew about spaceships, how they worked • Every day the junkies gather in front of my house • I didn't know we lived under a monarchy until I was 13 years old • My best friend in high school died of prettiness • Michelle sometimes longed for the days when astronomers like herself spent their time actually applying their eyeballs to the ends of telescopes pointed at the sky • Sometimes you have to deal with the world's troubles head on, which is why I have decided to run for county clerk, and I will tell you right here and now that no one is going to come close to stopping me, so don't even try, and forget about running against me, I'm going to gain the office unopposed • The mirror was supposed to give me access to the queen, but it did no such thing • My second trip to Scotland involved a denunciation of my first, for reasons I will go into but probably shouldn't • Dawn did a murder weekend every year, even though her friends were sick of it • You could measure my enthusiasm for the job by the angle of my boots, propped up as they were on the edge of my desk, and the set of my hat, tilted forward to keep the light out of my eyes • President Lincoln, I have decided, would not have liked my father • You shouldn't think I've seen it all, even though I've been to Cleveland • The band called me Doc because that's what Nuke named me way back when, but neither of us remembers why • Carol introduced herself to the audience by spelling her name as slowly as possible • Alvin drew his brand—an upside down A that got shaky after the stroke—on the first page of each Western he checked out from the library • Every kid loves shortcuts • Nothing rouses the senses like the barrel of a revolver pressed against your teeth • Mel asked his children where their mother was but none of them knew, and, more to the point, none of them cared • The bed held way more people than was reasonable • I was smart enough to begin a camel breeding operation in the American desert southwest, and I got nothing but ridicule for my efforts • My name was given to me by my parents, but I never liked Italo and changed it to Simon when I was five years old • No one wanted to eat the celery sticks, and who could blame them? • The dog announced itself with a piercing scream at my back door • I wouldn't call us a gang, not exactly • The thing that has always puzzled me is why the human naked body is so often associated with dread and danger • The steak was bloody and disgusting and I could not get enough of it • In the age of hysterics, old women consistently modeled sane behavior • I got a list of fears a mile long • The professor of aesthetics was droning on about disfiguring diseases being a kind of art form, which made Lance wonder what kind of school he had gotten himself into • Look, my parents had strange ideas about names and wanted something unpronounceable so they named me Qrfflxz and it wasn't until I was well into my teens that a judge made them change it to Linda • Corben was not the first one in his family to go to college, that distinction fell to his younger brother Gabe, but he was the first to make a million dollars • The fall came when no one was paying attention • No one knows the origins of a joke, any joke • The sky produced its own music • The sun being bright and hot on the day I was born, I was given the name Sol, which has confused most people who encounter it, thinking I must be named after some kind of fish • My out-of-body experience happened at just the right time to save my life • The row of tents in the passing lane of Interstate 5 should have been a dream, but it wasn't, a fact that made Forest's hands tremble with fear • I learned that my long lost cousin was actually living in the same city as me, and that he had found me, and that he wanted to hang out with me, damn the luck • My second husband became the proudest, most beautiful woman I had ever seen in my life • No such thing as a killer instinct, but I will say, from experience, there is such a thing as an instinct to kill • The Columbia River, severed by dams in more than a dozen places, resembles a series of reservoirs more than it does a living thing • I always feel like scooping up coins when I see them in fountains, but I've only done it a few times • The real issue about a tree falling in the forest is that it doesn't care if it makes a sound or not, it's dying • The neighbors were having a feast and didn't invite us • Edward Simpkins was just 12 years old when the invasion happened • Cars were killing us all, but we didn't care • Mrs Lister was not a cruel woman, but when the famished man appeared at her door asking for work and a bite to eat, she told him she was going to call the police and put the law on him if he didn't leave immediately • The grapes made me think of slick gravel, the sort of vision you didn't want in your head when you were preparing to steal them from the vines on your neighbor's property • Wendy first heard the ocean talk to her when she was two years old • Dex surprised the board by tendering his resignation exactly five minutes after he had been hired as the director of the Bureau of Surrealistic Research, although, all things considered, the board should have seen it coming • My wife left me after one week of marriage • A doctor's professional opinion, in my experience, isn't worth the prescription pad, emblazoned with a pharmaceutical logo, that it's scribbled on • Fathers die, that's a fact • Then I woke up and it wasn't a dream • The couple lived off the grid, squatting on land that wasn't theirs, eating food they found or stole, and sleeping more soundly than babies • My people, considered dirty liars by many, were the best storytellers I ever knew • The fourth round snuck up on me and lay me flat on the mat, a location that afforded, at least, some few seconds to contemplate my life decisions • I lost my little finger, which put me permanently off balance for the rest of my life • We mass-produced organs for transplant until the evangelicals put a stop to it • Late fame might be the best kind, but that didn't turn out to be much help to Max, who became the victim of a persistent stalker • The first ones struggled mightily that last year • For many years I refused to salt my food • My cat would not chase mice, ever, yet she lived in my house like a queen • All the mad people in the attic • You don't know hot unless you've spent some time in Tucson in the summer • The Marshall encountered the Ute while his horse was taking water from a creek at the bottom of a canyon he knew he shouldn't have entered • The water was covered in a slick gray *something,* but it didn't stop me from drinking it • My new shirt scraped against my skin like sandpaper, triggering a bad case of buyer's remorse • School had been out for less than two weeks when Shawn's mother died and Nelson went with him to the funeral home • Interiors don't always conform • First thing you have to know about me is that I hate dogs because they totally suck and don't even bother arguing with me about it because I have proof that no one can refute • In the end, my close relationship with the astrologer of the court did me no good at all • The house felt old • Everything looks good online until you buy it and the UPS guy drops it at your front door and you open the box and think *what idiot would buy something like this?* • My staff, all three souls, were not as committed to the lofty goals of the dispensary as I was, a fact that caused me no end of distress, much like a general in the field who laments the lackluster efforts of his soldiers, and worries that they will die, or, at the very least, be maimed and forced to live the rest of their lives in wheelchairs • Your kids will break your heart, count on it • My son Karl stole a candy bar from the convenience store a few blocks from our house • The simple stories are the best • Rhett's tear ducts got hooked up to a machine that required salt to operate • She didn't touch him or shake his hand • My story hardly bears repeating, but my killer thinks it worthy, so I'm going to set it down here while I still have breath and strength to do so •

I got lucky and became obscenely wealthy and people loved me for it until I gave it all away • The elevator doors opened onto a scene of carnage • Hate flourished in the ruins • My son grew up and began wearing glasses without lenses • Kate passed the hookah to her left, which meant I would have to wait till it went all the way around, which was no tragedy, but no highlight of my day either • I paid a compliment to the queen, which raised the ire of the king, who then banished me to the hinterlands where marauding bands of thieves tried to recruit me into their revolutionary project • Terra waited on the corner for several minutes, but the guy she had talked to on the phone never showed up • The foodies were a tiresome bunch • Creatures with claws were everywhere out there in the dark and it was all I could do to keep from screaming • I could have stayed longer, but the firm was changing for the worse, so I cashed in my stock options and retired before my thirtieth birthday • Once upon a time is no way to start a story, any story • He opened the door slowly, allowing the visitor to compose herself • For a while, until I divorced him, I had a husband who contradicted every single sentence I ever uttered • I lived in the palace, unnoticed, for 12 years • My income had been below the poverty line for some time and I was okay with that in a strange kind of way that frightened me with its complacency • It was the sort of day that sits back in a corner, the way a cat sometimes does, watching the proceedings, but not stepping up to participate, not yet • Glass marbles are keepers of worlds • It was a bright day, light streaming into the bedroom, and my bed-mate, my husband of more years than I care to admit, was not moving • I knew where Molly had hidden the axe • I've always thought people should be given provisional names until they are old enough to pick their own because then I wouldn't have been saddled with Elmer • Cal's umbrella looked like a bloodshot eye from above • I served mealworms to my guests and you'd have thought I had put plates of cow dung in front of them, such was their ridiculously animated and disgusted reaction • The investigators are inquiring into the nature of the storyteller, who has died • Everyone in the room wore a mask, which made it difficult to know who exactly I was hired to eliminate • My uncle was bald and said it was from worry so he told me when I was seven years old that I should never worry unless I wanted to be bald • If I could I would ride a meteor right into a planet, any planet, it wouldn't matter to me • Most of us have had the phone call from hell • Don't celebrate your birthday unless you want to • The traveler sought people who knew about the far side of things • The guy who kidnapped me, they say he's a monster, but he took care of me when I was six and he kept taking care of me until I was

11 and then he let me go and I was okay, mostly, so he's not a monster, exactly, but more of a mixed up guy, in my opinion • They call the procedure an autopsy, a strangely poetic and soothing word, to mask the brutality of what actually occurs during one • The diamond was a vulgar thing, bigger than an unshelled walnut, and I loved it • I've called the police a few times in my life and none of them ever helped the situation I was in • After we built the pyramid we sat in the sand and looked at it with admiration • All the guys in school wanted to see me naked • The hunters wore bright orange, which made me think they were members of some kind of cult that wanted to convert me • Alice looked through the large, concave blister to Earth, large and luminous in the sky • The road was narrow, which was bad enough, but also edged with a thousand foot drop unprotected by any guardrail • "Time traveller, huh?" said Helen • The stonemason cut handcrafted headstones of an exquisite workmanship but that did not keep him from losing his business when the stonecutting robot moved into town and worked so quickly and efficiently that it undercut his prices by more than half • Most of the miners I knew had foul mouths, it's true, but sometimes all they had was language to keep themselves alive, so they cultivated the most extreme examples they could • I was at that age when milk went from being a refreshing beverage

to a gloppy liquid you wouldn't want anywhere near your mouth • The apartment was pleasant enough, and the price was right, but I knew that at least one person had killed himself there, and that was a deal breaker and always would be • My father left me his stamp collection, his cat, and his debts • With a dry wind kicking up grits of sand into my face and hair, I stood on the dusty shore of the Nile River, my favorite spot on the planet • My octopus loved me • Cory's face, hands, calves, shoulders, and back all bore tattooed versions of the flag, just so no one would mistake him for a non-patriot • The family was dressed in rags, but they wore them well • Dawn can make predators of any of us at a moment's notice • I kept "assassin" off my resume because, well, you know • Beds are the fertility grounds of mankind • The dead body on the road was starting to rot • When I was five years old an alien ate my father • The deputy was in trouble but whether he knew it or not was still an open question • The house was gutted • Al yearned to be an identical, rather than a fraternal, twin, a wish shared by his twin sister • "Forensics," said Detective Wren to the parents of the young victim, "is not like on TV and is harder than it looks so what is really necessary is that someone who saw her daughter get killed should come forward and tell his or her story" • The robot, I was almost one hundred percent sure, was a virgin • We were modern day cannibals, so no giant pots of missionary soup for us because elegance is so much more conducive to an enjoyable dining experience • The War of the Brothers began when one of them refused to return a pair of shears he had borrowed from the other • When Senaway was still a child, she learned about the aging trek from her mother • Don't devote your life to literature • Joe named his boat *The Joe* because he liked things that reminded him of himself • I'm very wary of quick friendships, so when I travel by train I avoid human contact as much as possible and keep to myself and my room • Each witness wore a white shirt and a black tie and both of them had giant invisible leeches stuck to their backs and neither of them knew it • I saw my share of playground fights when I was a kid, but I never waded into that particular sewer until November of eighth grade • We found the place mat in the bottom of the chest of drawers • Arranged marriages, I know from personal experience, are better than arranged births • The argument was about butts, which movie hunk had the best one, but, really, we were only killing time until the verdict was announced and we could go on air and tell the world whether Burt Magnus was a bona fide killer or just a poor slob wrongfully accused • Go to the edge of the Earth, where the water spills off into the void • Howard's notebook was the only thing left in the apartment, besides Howard's body, of course • Derek decided Dvorak devotees didn't deserve double duty • Sometimes you think you're alone when you're not • I had not had a meal in many months • I never fasten my seat belt when I'm on a plane because by not doing so I inevitably invite the attentions of flight attendants, who are often very pretty • The spider was in the bottom of his cup • Abel was at a board meeting when he saw the tornado warning slide across his phone • The whole feeling in the rain forest was of arrested motion • I like the street fair not only because for a few days each summer the main downtown streets are closed to traffic and given over to those on foot, but also because of the unlikely mix of people I always find there: aging hippies in beads and Birkenstocks, business folks in dark severe suits, beggars with their hand out, suburban families, flakes, junkies, artists, nerds, and bikers • I was poor, which was bad, but even worse was that I had children, growing children, who refused to do any work around the house or the shop • The carrots sent up fountains of green in my garden, as though the orange underneath wanted a showy announcement before presenting itself to the world • Pamela Kipling, high school teacher, loves the bottle and it loves her back • Some cities are just naturally dark • Most of my work I complete in a few days, but the sculpture of the king took me more months than I care to admit, even though there was good reason for it • God made me so ugly that people could not look at me • The smoke harvest was gloriously bountiful that year • We all carry portals into other worlds • Margaret Rock put the president's life above her own, even above her own family • The turtles • Angels are a touchy bunch • Even days after Icarus died, feathers kept falling from the sky, stately, silent, and tipped with clumps of melting wax • I showed Faber the picture, never expecting him to tear it to shreds in front of my eyes • The trail was littered with wrecked wasp nests • After the war some of the soldiers refused to go home • I rode my horse hard for days until blood sprayed out of her nostrils and I knew she was finished • Well-cooked rice was a project that always defeated me • The rainbow sheen on a fresh piece of tuna, like an oil slick on a sidewalk • My skin color went from normal to a kind of half-fluorescent reddish-green in a matter of a few weeks • The easiest thing to say about that day was that it started out so nice, what with the birds singing, the sun giving an early morning glow to everything, and the fragrance of lavender everywhere • All told, the theft took about 30 days • I was the wicked stepsister • Everyone thinks they have good taste and very few people actually do • Lisa's voting party took place in the upper reaches of an all-but-abandoned high rise down by the waterfront • The second time I faced a firing squad I really hoped they wouldn't miss like the first one had • The poison in the apple pie was not immediately obvious and would not become so for another 24 hours when the first of Gwen's victims experienced acute pain in his heart • My parents said I was a surprise, which told me I was more or less an accident • Gart said he was going to burn the town down and by the look of the smoke plume rising, he was as good as his word • The bathroom was tiled in alternating pink and purple squares • You can be a hero in your family's eyes, but it is not the same kind of hero the public wants and will sometimes transform you into • Ed shook his head to clear his skull of the dense fog that always seemed to fill his brain after several hours of keyboarding • Hart's apartment was at the assisted living center but not because he was old • Listen, you can be as bohemian as you like, living on the edge by your wits and telling the world to go fuck itself, but, in the end, you gotta eat, just like everyone else • Bryson never felt guilty about striking it rich in the dot com boom and lording it over all the poor slobs who labored endlessly to no avail • When I got out of prison, baths were the thing that scared me the most • As soon as people learn that they did not originate on this planet, they come to me • Parliament Hill sometimes feels like the center of a small provincial town, which is what it is • The tower rose up from the desert floor like a needle about to prick the balloon of heaven

• Eustace C Filmore III, musical genius, spent his days locked up in his parent's basement, practicing the piano for hour after hour • Holt bored his neighbors by constantly telling stories of his war exploits • The oval office is a cage • According to most folks in my adopted home, I come from an exotic and beautiful country, but I know better • I'll start with small words so you can understand • I had three very competent and ambitious sons, which was a problem because they had their sights on my company and I didn't want to see it go out of my hands • My first love was not a person, an animal, or a thing • I give two dollars to the first panhandler I see on any given day, but that's it, that's my limit • I'm at home, in my apartment above Broadway, when I hear the crash of metal colliding and the splintering of glass breaking and the crushing sound of someone calling out for help, anguished like, but I don't get up off my couch because, well, because I also hear sirens on the way and how exactly could I help things anyway, being a confined criminal with a monitor on my ankle? • I had the right to remain silent • The dish was called Beelzebub's Chicken, which made me wonder if the devil was in all of us • I had a magic tea kettle • The one thing I learned is that it was not so bad living without a brain • Once you understand that cooking destroys the vitality of all food, you will see my life for what it is: an attempt to educate the masses • Before

I finished the wedding cake—I was only a few dollops of icing from the end—this *light* illuminated everything: the cake, my hand, the icer, the *air* • After I emigrated from Gwanderly to Canada I did everything I could to keep my former countrymen out of my adopted home • One of my plants radiated an overly large and aggressive aura • I had a pet turtle for many years until it turned vicious • Four natives are my family now • The lifeboat was listing badly to one side and I was about to bring up the question of who of us should go overboard and how were we to decide, when my eight-year-old daughter asked me if we were going to get our money back for this trip that was, in her words, "totally fucked up" • My two husbands were not getting along • I was just a little kid the first time we moved, so I wasn't prepared when the house we were leaving tried to hold me back • Cassandra was convinced no one really like parties, but just pretended and hoped no one noticed • Linc told anyone who would listen about the time he was shot in the face • Everyone knew professor Walinsky was a genius, but I was one of the few who also knew him to be a mad, raving lunatic • The room captured the essence of what it meant to be old and incapacitated in the early years of the twenty-first century • Once you shoot the President, your life is not your own • Most of the land was flooded with bodies floating by and snagging debris like ghastly islands of rotting vegetation • The spinning wheel, once Rose got it working properly, produced sufficient quantities of gold for her to quit her job and become a woman of both leisure and seclusion, which suited her just fine • Brothers will always be rivals • My story is your story • On the morning of his monthly alter day, Bryon avoided gauging his mood, preferring to allow his environment time to affect his actions • We will need to talk about food for a long time • Constance is not a name you normally associate with someone born in the late 20th century, but from the start I was an oddball and an outcast • Judy was wrapped around Kira Ametite's hand while Ron Soririac, the best Punch in puppetry, stood beside her • Everyone thinks your weight is their business • During the occupation a lot of us lived in holes in the ground just to survive • I unrolled the scroll with shaking hands • To tell you the truth, I was never sure which was worse: hospitals or prisons • Murder is good for business • Maia kept everyone away from the crime scene for five minutes, intending to feel the vibes of the place, but only got confused images that told her nothing about the man at her feet who, from all appearances, bled out from a knife wound to his neck • I was a famous accordionist, which is a little like being a famous checkers player, which is to say, not famous at all • Bell's robot thought it was way smarter than it really was and Bell liked to tell it that over and over • I used to fight for justice for my people, but now I mostly give interviews about my younger days, those years when killing others for a better world was considered expedient and right and would not land you in jail, where I am now • The chief occupation of people is clerical—putting things (themselves, especially) where they belong • We were rich and we liked to throw lavish parties and some of the neighbors found fault with that • I was small, which meant that I could disappear into the background of the world, just like old women sometimes do, and get exactly what I wanted • No one knew exactly what young Oren's father was dying of, but everyone heard the discomforting screams of the dying man • I never wanted to enter the cave • From his chair on the other side of the table, Nichols looked like the peaceful sort of person who might spend his evenings doing wood carvings or origami • If God gives you insomnia, he should also give you something interesting to do in the middle of the night, otherwise he's just being a jerk • The fight was a more or less friendly thing with no weapons, just some guys letting off steam, when one of the little guys on the other side retreated to his car and returned with a knife • Ash from the volcano fell around me like strange warm snow • Don always thought my passion for knitting was an aberration • My birth surprised everyone except me • All the giants were deaf • I welcomed the return of the missing bishop • Alex opened the book to the middle section, where the pictures were • A time lapse film of the full moon during those years would have shown a bright silver disk fading gradually to black • Tyler caught up with the thief just as she tried to duck into the subway • They called Alfred Doctor Al just because he carried a black bag and smiled broadly at anyone who was even a little bit sick • After the riot, Rose felt exhilaration tempered with a pinch of regret for some of what she did • Whenever Hailey had a question she needed answered, she did not turn to Google, but instead called the local public library where a nice young man usually answered the phone and was only too happy to tell her the spelling of *reverence,* or look up the side effects of fentanyl, or find for her the latest discoveries in the field of UFO research • If you don't already know that telepaths completely suck as friends then I honestly don't think I can help you or even talk to you • I don't talk so good but I be a hella smart guy, yup • Nate proposed to me in a crowded restaurant with many of the other diners looking on with studied amusement • Lottery winners think their shit doesn't stink • We named my sister Katrina because the day she was born was the day that hurricane hit New Orleans and she's been a source of fury and disruption ever since • Pamela stood on the hilltop and faced the storm and turned it away • My name has been Robin all my life, but I think if I had to be associated with a bird I would have named myself Eagle instead • I never developed a taste for fish • After the world ended there were a lot of folks who wanted to keep going and I had to wonder why • I had read Nenad Dragicevic's epidermal narrative (a term he invented) in its original form, literally on the backs of working people, when his troupe of tattooed pages toured the west coast • You won't find our town on the map, any map, though you can stumble over it in real life, rather like stubbing your toe on a rock • Passing is not good for the soul but if you do it long enough your soul more or less evaporates and everything is tolerable after that • My phone rang and indicated the caller was Diablo, but I don't take phone calls from hell, never have, never will • Simple folk, I'm sure you've heard of them, are even simpler than you can imagine • The landlord didn't like me but he liked my rent checks • The android had bruises on her face and shoulders • I was fourteen, old enough, apparently, to learn something of our history • Love and death, certainly, but not necessarily in that order • Whenever Eve took her six children out in public she got dirty looks from just about everybody she met • From my bedroom window I can see the scaffolding being built by my neighbors • The ocean healed me • I never much liked whales, or the unthinking admiration they seemed to attract from so many • The kid had this hitch in his aura, a sure sign he wasn't going to last much longer • The king no longer had a kingdom • When we played chess Craig called the black pieces niggas, and even though I told him to knock it off, I knew he didn't mean anything by it • In the old days, before all of this, James used to like to play a little game • You know what I mean • The new sheriff of Happenstance, Arizona, was from Maine, unused to the heat here, and I gave him two weeks, tops, before he wilted and slunk back to the east coast where he obviously belonged • The first snowstorm of winter brought silence after a season of unspeakable carnage • Antarctica doesn't give a shit about you and your will to live • I'm going to say this slowly and carefully and only once so pay attention and ignore the water rising up to our chins because there's nothing we can do about that • My cousin told me live is evil spelled backwards, like that meant something • Don't call me a potato head • I envy people with simple names and simple lives, like my friend Bev • Everyone thinks I'm happy, and I am, but it still bothers me that no one ever *asks* how I'm doing • One morning Kathy's younger brother Brian turned into a giant—*ick*—cockroach, and, even worse, was that her parents said *she had to take care of him* • Wilson Murchie pulled back the gleaming clear door of the hospital entrance and stepped from a cold Michigan February into the warm and antiseptic atmosphere of the hospital corridor • Jessica was disturbed by her conversation with Marion, especially as it came just before her renewal hearing in front of the immortality board • Has the net yielded up what you need? • The prince was a complete asshole • Bruce didn't want a retirement party, but his staff put one on for him anyway, much to his embarrassment and quiet rage • When I was 12 my parents apprenticed me to a carpenter, who turned out to be not only a tyrant but a violent one as well • Daughters have all the power in a family • I'm not the sort of guy who thinks my hometown is great just because it's my hometown, but, well, it *is* great • My home planet is a gas giant • The worst time for a garbage disposal to malfunction is three a.m. on a Sunday morning • They wanted to test me for drugs, like I was some sort of criminal • Reclusive sound engineer Kristine Manfred had a secret that allowed her to live a cushy life scoring sound tracks for big budget Hollywood movies • My Uber driver suffered a heart attack while going ten miles over the speed limit on I-5, in the heart of Seattle, with 18-wheelers on either side of us • My siblings, being named Kyle, Karen, Kate, and Keith, set up a pattern, which I broke by being named Theresa and that simple fact has troubled me all my life • He went underground that morning, just another miner doing his job, except this time, when he came back to the surface, there was something different about him • The guy lived on top of a mountain, like he was some kind of oracle instead of the prime suspect in my first murder case • My first time in Montreal didn't go nearly as well as I had hoped • Orphans always recognize each other • After my first killing I expected a sense of satisfaction mixed with guilt but instead all I got was numbness and a need to run away from the scene while there was still time • Princess Ristour's destiny was to be king • Lawyers, it is rumored, are people just like you and me, but as one of them might say in court: *show me the evidence for that contention* • The search was in its seventh day when you could feel hope begin to slip away from just about everyone on our team • The guy was wearing a suit, so I didn't believe a thing he said • After a long night of coding, with the sun just lightening the eastern sky, I stepped out of headquarters and was aware of a change in the world which was subtle, but strong enough to give my whole system an adrenaline jolt I did not expect • I fell asleep on the bus and missed my stop by several horrors • My mail needed polishing to remove the rust, and my lance had splintered, and my horse was old, tired, and nasty, but I was still a knight, dammit, and I had a maiden to rescue, if I only knew where she was being held captive • And then I became a star • We used to beg my parents to tell stories of the old country, but they never did • When I was just 11 years old my friends and I, wandering around in the woods behind my house, found a dead guy covered with just a few inches of leaves and branches and a little bit of dirt, like some dog had kicked him there • We had been best friends—good best friends—for so many years that we understood the lies between us and welcomed them as the purest kind of authenticity • In the gig economy my life as a tailor took on a more or less folklorish patina • In our school, if you had a foreign name like Torq or Choto or Sheng or Bakari you were going to get the shit pounded out of you, count on it • I never felt good about eating vegetables • The oil painting, which depicted the back of a watercolor painting, was not for sale • My best feature was the scar that started under my left ear, wormed its way across my cheek, crawled between my nose and upper lip, crossed the gulf of my mouth, and ended in a short nasty tail just north of the right side of my chin • I carried fire with me always • In the big inning • Some days it feels good to leave all the dishes piled up in the sink all dirty and gross • The wax museum in Carson City had a model of me that was not very well done • I used to imagine God and Satan as rival quarterbacks for teams that met once each season for an epic battle that lasted for days and attracted die hard fans on both sides, the kind that would engage in brawls at the drop of a helmet • The logo on the front door reminded me of a pile of dog droppings, prompting me to wonder if this is really where I wanted to work • I was a simpleton in those days, or pretended to be, for the express purpose of having people tell me their secrets • Alone with her thoughts, he sipped his coffee in the quiet lunch room of Carrier's Inc • Jasmine never told anyone about what she did at the department of corrections because no one would believe her • My view of elephants changed after one of them—a bull named Charlie—asked me about my plans for the weekend • The headlights coming toward me looked angry • It was my wife's idea for us to split up, but it was all my fault • Hope is for fools • Janson Heard devised a method of washing clothes that involved no water or solvents of any kind • At the Tao of Tea the seaweed spoke to every diner, even those who did not order the sushi • The elephants looked slightly out of place in my front yard • The doctor said my heart was too big • The president found the body behind the palace and stuck a straw into it and sucked up enough fluid to fully and completely understand his people and what they wanted • I had some money, for once • When the ocean turned blood red, I figured it was time to go inland • Some people keep their culture, others try to ignore it, and still others will do anything necessary to kill it • Poor people are different than you and moi • On the island we were not used to strangers and were unsure of how to kill one when he arrived unannounced, unshaven, and unclean • I don't guess, I *know* when a spot will be hit by lightning, even if it's a hundred years in the future, or a million • For my birthday I wanted a spaceship, and that's what I got • When she got to be around 75, my mother's walks became epic, traversing the whole city and taking three or four hours to complete • The smell of jasmine in the air doesn't remind me of anything in particular, but it does fill me up with hope • Time wounds all heels • You own a six-shooter, well, you're okay by me • We met cute, which was fine, but I still had to kill him • The plane hiccuped, then faltered, and, finally, began spinning • Bigfoot is a fairy • Every town, from the tiniest hamlet to the largest metropolis, has places no one should go if they want to hold onto their sanity • Rivals don't have to kill each other • Vern spent two hours making himself up to look like he had no makeup • Travis preferred carrier pigeon over email, and whether you found this ridiculous or charming pretty much determined how you felt about Travis • The right lane was about to end and I couldn't get over • The instant of death is an illusion • Names are like ghosts that attach themselves to your life and there is no joy in being yoked to the name Delbert • The bird was dying, so no wonder I was angry • For Henna's eighth birthday, her parents got her a blimp, even though what she really wanted was a time machine • The song of the world is more nursery rhyme than opera • When I was a kid, the forest behind my house was filled with spirits that loved me • The trail to death began at the pond and wound through the rising forest floor along the creek to higher elevations, then up past the edge of the melting glaciers, across the talus fields, and up even further to the summit of the mountain, although few pilgrims actually got that far since most were cut down at the lower elevations by starvation, injury, or the teeth of ravenous animals • I always thought of my nose ring as a device to snag my soul if it ever chose to try to leave me • The wind in my part of the world is an angry thing, ready to snatch you up and hurl you against a tree • Mark ate breakfast quietly, unlike the other members of his family • My father died first, then my mother soon after, and neither of them left me any words of wisdom to guide me through life • The doctor wasn't my idea of competent • When Earth was still flat and the fertile sky had not yet sprouted stars, a bird the color of new flesh landed on Bryn's head and whispered into her ear that a baby was about to be born under a quarter moon at the edge of the world • In early spring we used to pull out our marbles and play on any piece of ground where the snow had melted enough to reveal some brown and matted patch of grass • I found the body at a particularly low point in my life • Frood Road looped up over Sudbury through blackened rockscapes and then descended to a dusty section of town and ended as a narrow street lined with broken wooden houses that looked like rows of teeth that needed dental work • The rain kept me up all night • Too many murder victims to count • I wanted a view of paradise but got a front seat to carnage instead • My parents loved Shakespeare and I paid the price because they named me Cordelia • In our school it was understood that no one said anything bad about Sparky Anderson • The interior of a found golf ball, when you are six years old, is a mystery that absolutely needs to be uncovered • The day Curt met the new couple next door was also the day they were murdered • The box of cotton balls had holes poked in the sides, as though someone had taken a sharp instrument and punctured the thin cardboard several times • I have always been fond of disasters • When I moved into the house, I kept getting mail for the previous tenant, lots of political propaganda of a distasteful nature that made me think it was all well and good that the old guy was dead • They wouldn't take me for the war because they said I was too old • Impending death casts a clarifying light on many things, but, it turns out, not on the mystery of life • Her green eyes held flecks of silver • When I tell people my name is Bonnie, they often ask me if

I lie over the ocean and I just want to slug them • The streets were flooded and salmon swam by stop signs and speed bumps • First came love, then came marriage, then the wind, ice, wild fires, and flooding • Faye set the reality outside her window to a Mars scape, but it kept flickering to a staticky Titan which annoyed her because Titan had its problems and always would • The comma bothered me a lot but there was little I could do about it • The chronotree had ripe fruit before it was mature enough to do so, a fact that turned me into a true believer • The freighter arrived too late to be unloaded that night, so we had to wait until the morning • In a blackened softness where he felt no sensations, Clive Lockhart began his third gestation in as many months • Unlike *them* I can remember my birth • Listen, kids like us, we play all the time to fool us into thinking things are okay when we know they aren't, not really • My shoes needed polishing • There is nothing stranger than pure normalcy • My royal heritage was kept from me until I was 19, long after I had grown to detest the very people—kings, queens, princesses and princes—who turned out to be my family members • The firefly's glow wasn't right • When Edmund jumped to Maspero last year I wanted to go with him but he said I wasn't ready • Back in the day, Herman dabbled in the sciences, producing some minor results of interest to a small group of fellow scientists, but years later decided instead that his calling was elsewhere and devoted his life to being the best sports mascot he could be • The stars were not following their usual track, accounting for the rush of fear coursing down my spine • The weirdest thing we found in Aunt Ladda's effects was a collection of about a thousand salt and pepper shakers that she had, apparently, pilfered from various restaurants over the course of her long life • I had really long hair, almost like Rapunzel in the fairy tale, and the guy who cut it was named Prince and he didn't get why that was charming, which I found more disappointing than I can say • My Dad liked riding his motorcycle so much that sometimes, when he came into the house, he kept his helmet on and wouldn't take it off even if my mother begged him to • The itch on his inner forearm—where he had gotten a black widow tattoo years ago—would not go away • I'm not going to respect your religion, okay? • I hear people say *prolly* instead of *probably* all the time and it makes me crazy • The couple who moved in next door to Grace had dogs, which was against the rules of the building • Yeah, I spend my days shadowing guys whose wives think they're cheating and if you have a problem with that, well, maybe you shouldn't read anymore of what I'm about to tell you • They gave me eyes but didn't explain how to use them • For a year I set up my booth in front of city hall and I would do your caricatures for ten dollars and that was how I made a steady income for those twelve months until the city decided I was a nuisance and rousted me out of there • The onions made me cry tears fatter than the biggest raindrops I had ever seen • The tugboats on the river are switching direction, trading barges • A successful pillow fight requires tactical expertise, the will to kill, and a devotion to righteousness at all costs • The Indians put the drop on us, killing five before we even knew what was happening, and sending the rest of us scurrying for cover from their arrows which pin-pricked the air and brought visions of salvation to my eyes • What was infuriating was the careful documentation of the extinction when it would have been far better for all those scientists to actually *do* something to try to reverse the plague • I have a diversified portfolio valued in the tens of millions of dollars, but I declare with all the humility I can muster that I am at heart a simple man with simple tastes • Bibi always pretended she was fine, most especially after she had been diagnosed with terminal leukemia • One time I was at Lano's house watching the space channel • Lawrence wasn't much of teacher, but he looked the part, with his prominent glasses, studious features, and a demeanor that invited trust and seemed to hide reservoirs of knowledge which, truth be told, weren't actually there • You folks made a mistake • Trust me when

I say the one thing, the *one* thing, you don't want is to know what people are thinking • Arson is its own reward • People tell me they think my profession is morally indefensible, but I gotta tell ya, torturers have feelings too, and that kind of talk just hurts me more deeply than I can say • Ralph Tweet did not like his names • When I travel I like to eat strange things • I threw up before and after my first concert, but, fortunately, not *during*, a fact I took as a victory • My first time on a horse broke me • The social contract has too many articles, in my opinion • I did the calculation: 8 billion people on the planet, average lifespan about 70 years, so a human death approximately every three and a half seconds • Incest always hurts someone • My family rarely thought of me as a fool • My story begins and ends in the same place: Stonehenge • I was, frankly, bored of the flies, all of them • When you're in a country unfamiliar to you, the locals often get stuck on your name, trying to pronounce it, but mangling it terribly, and making you think the fault lies with you and your ridiculous name, even if it's something simple like Carl • Freeze frames are lies, pure and simple • The body was male, nude, wrapped in plastic, obviously mutilated, and had absolutely no aura of mystery or danger, a fact I ascribed to my jaded nature, having seen too many such victims already • Listen, it's not my fault that a man's neck invites my hands to wrap themselves around it, not my fault at all that such an action evokes a sublime feeling of power mixed with pleasure • Marriage is not so much a partnership as it is a mutual hostile takeover • The salad here is always bitter • Everett's spirit animal was a bipolar bear • Dorren forged great iron bells for a living, but lately no one was much interested in bells and had taken to asking Dorren for bicycles, a task she flatly refused for many years, until her hunger got the better of her • Don't tell me your dreams, ever • I felt sorry for the guy on the park bench who was clearly distraught, but I didn't do anything to comfort him • Nothing like a hospital waiting room for highlighting the boredom and terror lurking behind every instant of life • A cool autumn afternoon in Vermont, crisp and sunny, was an inviting and lovely backdrop for the tall maple that had turned magnificent shades of red, yellow, and orange • I lived with a chess player who lived only for chess • My aunt said the new baby was born with a devil's curse on her • Najet's neighbors didn't like that she kept chickens and goats • You can work hard all your life, but I found a better way to live and it's only mildly immoral • The kitten in the tree, for me, was more symbol than it was a call to action • Tending to the hurts of others does a soul good, so they say • Some journeys are necessary, others thrust upon you • He had the look of someone who thought he was still thin • The ceiling fan was a spinning asterisk • Swimming heads • A lot of people didn't understand what the visitors from the stars really wanted from us • Don't ask me my name, not if you value your life • Before he got old and resembled a burnt out filament, he was actually, for a short time, the light of my life • The tattoo studio was sandwiched between an adult bookstore and a topless bar • Mature people are boring • I think I was about eight years old when I realized that some grownups hate children enough to kill them, or worse, abandon them • Traffic was a complete fluster cluck • The Bridge of the Gods is visible from miles away, a toy assemblage of cantilevered beams, silver and dazzling against the dark green cliffs that tower on either side of the Columbia River • My car hated me • After the invasion, our town was the first to go • I wanted to do a musical of hurricane Irma but my cast voted that down in favor of an all singing all dancing show based on the first responders to the explosion at Oklahoma City in 1995 • My goats hated me • I caught my tenth grade English teacher looking me up and down and he wasn't even embarrassed, which was way messed up • Migrating birds, tiny things, often stopped at the lighthouse for a short rest and I always put out birdseed for them • Kara, once she realized most people were faking their way through life, decided she would do the same • The salmon liked to gather their strength in the placid pools of the bay before beginning their journey up the river to their spawning grounds • Doors have no sense of right or wrong • I break into people's houses and because of that the law says some jerk can shoot me and it's just my tough luck if I die • Disheveled hair is no sin, but neither is it a sign of saintliness • My grandma, who never wanted to get old, used to tell me having a 90th birthday was in very poor taste • Being a doctor is a calling for some, but for me it was just a job • The Rio Grande River was a fine border and we loved riding next to it • Some guys in town, they think rustlers don't deserve the death penalty, but most of us, the sensible ones, know they are dead wrong • After some harrowing days reporting on the atrocities in Bosnia, it was, to my shame, depressingly easy to return home and worry about making the mortgage and arranging to fix the scratch on my car and getting on the phone and negotiating a better price on my cable subscription • The aliens made excellent slaves, and since they had no legal standing there were no moral issues involved • The hull was covered with shellfish and would have to spend days in dry dock getting cleaned up and seaworthy, time I did not have • Violet always knew, from the time she was five, when the grownups were lying • The king's shadow was in my pocket, folded up into a compact ball, which was the more or less accepted way to transport a shadow • Deb drew the short straw, so she became the kid who was going to walk up to the over-lords and ask them "What up?" • I got nothing and lots of people got so much but none of them will share with me, not a single one • Kevin examined the restaurant's menu, which was printed in brown ink on paper that simulated a graying, antique look • We put the beers in the creek to keep them cold, then forgot about them until the next day • I used to write fan letters to architects • Lots of people think they have power, but practically no one does • Peter pressed his hand to the burner and felt no warmth • My father used to kill people then come home and tell me about it but he stopped the year I turned 16 and wrote up his activities in a notebook instead • Vampires are so yesterday • He had short fin-gers for a pianist • Don't get in the way of any two finalists at a chili cook off, that's all I'm saying • I was a foundling, which sounds like I'm from a fairy tale or the 14th century or something, but no, I was born after the first tower was hit and before the second one swal-lowed that plane like it was a fish in an ocean of air • Val's shadow clung to his body most of his life • I liked being a monk for about four days, then it all went downhill for me and never went back up • The tornado loved me • My congregation thought I was a piece of shit • Sick people should keep to themselves • I never thought of myself as a loser until last night • The local legend was that the water tower held the spirits of all the dead child molesters from our town, which only goes to show how messed up local legends can be • She smelled like the air does just as it's beginning to rain • I never told anyone my birthday, ever, and keeping it a secret served me well for many years • The campsite gave no indication that it had been occupied by murder victims • When I moved to Canada I couldn't find anyone who spoke my native language and felt such intense grief at its loss that I turned to drink and spoke my mother tongue to shadows, dream figures, and floating apparitions • My worst job was the summer I collected all the dead birds that fell after flying into the glass tower my family built in the middle of town • My father viewed the dinner table as something approaching a debate stage, in which we were pressed to express and defend our opinions, even if, like me, I mostly just wanted to eat in silence • My father should have stayed and raised us, I guess, but he had other plans and I can't begrudge him his dreams, no matter how much, for a long time, I really wanted to • The bug arrived at my house uninvited, as most bugs do, one warm spring morning • Even his father and mother adopted blank expressions when Adex asked what was happening to their world • Babies ruin everything • I was so thin my wrist watch kept falling off and crashing to the floor, sending up a clatter that assaulted my ears • My punishment was out of proportion to my crime, or so my lawyer, unsuccessfully, argued • I couldn't tell if the clock showed 11:05 or 12:55 and I wasn't sure if it mattered • Watermelons are such crazy things I sometimes think they shouldn't exist • I want to be more like cats • As a rule, actors don't make good spouses • The letter, just by *being* a letter in the second decade of the twenty-first century, was highly suspicious and I put off opening it for several days • All the sand has fallen through to the bottom of the hour glass • My car was talking to me and I didn't like what it was saying • Unable to sleep through the noise of the Oregon storm outside, David Suits rolled out of bed and felt his way in the dark to the bedroom door • The nineteenth century turned out to be more pleasant than I had expected • Barry shouldn't have entered the apartment, he knew that, but the door, ajar as it was, proved to be an irresistible temptation • The neighbor's house had been dark for several nights and I was working up the courage to walk over and knock on the door and inquire as to what might be going on when the police arrived and surrounded both our houses • You get to know a person, down in the ground • I found the severed hand where I least expected it and realized immediately how odd it was that I expected to find a severed hand anywhere • No one, no matter how bad they are, should be forced to remember their death • My mustache had a life of its own • Her hair haunted my dreams • I never went to Paris but I watched every movie set in Paris that I could find, even the animated ones and the ones that weren't set in Paris but were filmed there, a delicious irony, I always thought, because it mirrored my own failure to get there • The ice at Daniel's feet was black and his breath hung in the air for an instant, a white cloud, then disappeared into nothing • I knew I had to get out of the tornado's path, but the truth is that I was too tired to move so I took my chances and stayed in my house • One day a man received a package by UPS • The fish that year were emaciated • Einstein in my dreams, every night for weeks, telling me he made a mistake and he's sorry, but the universe loved him and he loved it back and can't I understand that, for the love of all that's right, can't I see that's how it had to be? • The devil donned a mask and walked about the world, unnoticed, looking for some clues to understanding the wickedness of ordinary people • See, the thing is, how can we all be happy and prosperous and everything, when there's people getting killed by drones because someone ten thousand miles away pushes a button then goes home to his or her family and eats dinner and reads his or her daughter a bedtime story, then watches television and goes to bed and sleeps soundly? • His name was Pest • The prisoner I was transporting had a lot of stories about his years killing Indians

• The sleeping bags, piled up high in the corner, looked like camouflaged marshmallows • During roll call I always felt like my name was the odd one in the bunch, which didn't suit me at all • I was in an unfamiliar part of the country and did not understand the Creek's dialect • English's rampant ambiguity defeated us awl • The passengers tried to revive Professor Hagsden, who was slumped over in seat 12B, but it was no use • Rupert never met Isabelle, my wife, until after he died • Canadians say grade nine, not ninth grade • I'm a judge with magical powers, a fact you must accept if the following narrative is going to make any sense at all • The place where I usually got my halo polished had closed up shop • My assignment was to find the legendary lost continent and make it safe for commerce • Suits are jerks • The Sea Cliffs Bed and Breakfast was an old gray house decorated in greenish moss, situated a half mile off highway 101 on the Oregon coast midway between California and Washington, and it was a haven for seagulls, who visited often and left whitish streaks like rows of picket fencing down the slope of the roof • The princess was expected to choose a husband from among her many suitors, but was not inclined to attach a man to her life and declined to entertain any offers, which filled her mother, the queen, with a mixture of anger and respect, a situation that had to resolve itself one way or the other if the country was to prosper • The steady rain in our town, coming down in torrents for days at a time, beats on roofs long and hard enough to eclipse a person's heartbeat • My job was to name all the new species the scientists kept finding • Each day is the same • We were good neighbors until the Wallaces planted that damned tree • I was with the president when he shot himself, clumsily, I might add, so I had to finish the job for him, as he begged me to do • I keep a distance from the city, but that night it snaked into my apartment and looked around for a nice place to sit, like a distasteful visitor I wanted gone • The serpent's gaze had its virtues, I won't deny it • The flock of butterflies took their time coming toward Mercury • It was a dire sitch, no doubt, me without my weapon and three dudes pointing guns at me, but even so, I couldn't help noticing the chiseled features of the guy on the left, not to mention his dark curly hair and his awesomely charming smile • Boxers, even before they get punch drunk, are idiots • Nothing more pathetic than an 85-year-old revolutionary • When Cori got scared she didn't feel it in her heart or her spine or her knees, but in her eyes • Stone soup makes a lot of sense • Casual has its attractions, I suppose, but for the sake of maintaining social order, I prefer formal attire and formal address • My midlife crisis hit me late, just around my hundredth birthday • First Shlegal, then me • Gladys never understood why people killed their spouses instead of getting a divorce, but that all changed after six years of her matrimonial union to Alan • We cut our palms and pressed them together so we could be blood brothers, whatever that was • I still have pictures of me when every guy wore a hat because that's what all guys did • A fish, like a leg, is all muscle • Hal's mother held him up in the apartment window so he could look down at the parking lot where his father drove up in a brand new black Ford station wagon • When I tended bar, there weren't too many folks who knew I once made cocktails of the Molotov type • Being rich is a burden but no one wants to hear that • I think we have wishful thinking because for many of us, when we were kids, wishes really did come true • The house had red walls and floors painted a curious shade of orange, like it was unsure if it wanted to actually *be* orange or maybe strive for something a little less obvious • The flypaper was so thick with the disgusting insects, their wings, legs, and heads all jammed together in a mucky orgy of grotesque porridge, that it made me sick • Wings are a pain in the ass • I didn't get the part, but I did sleep with the casting direc-tor, so you can think of me as either lucky or a slut, your pick • The sun was bigger in the sky than it should have been • The horns didn't bother me at first, but then I tried putting on my hat • The young woman chose her moment, then approached Prime Minister Sheila Gunderson holding what appeared to be a knife in one hand and a pen in the other • Rise up • Mason Dust lifted the cover of the photocopier, placed his typewritten chain letter on the glass, and closed the cover over it • Listen, you can kill birds by keeping them in the sky, not letting them alight anywhere, because then they can't eat and they die of starvation trying to keep their wings going • Sure I hated Andora, but not enough to kill her • The hurricane ate my hometown like it was a small appetizer • The shoes lifted me into the air and kept me there for long enough so that I knew these were the ones, these were the magic shoes my grandfather told me about • The life jacket, once I put it on, turned out to be so old that it disintegrated in my hand, which, given the rising water, gave me a bit of a fright • Desire proves nothing • Don't talk to me about happy families; they don't exist and never have • It wasn't exactly love at first sight because it took us more than forty years to get married after our first meeting on the sinking ferry • The international space station, a truly disappointing real life version of the space stations I imagined when I was a kid, did cast a stunning shadow against the sun, I will admit *that* • A pigeon flew overhead, about three feet away—something of a close call for airborne life • No one expects to be kidnapped by Indians, certainly not me • The crying man used to have friends, but that was before he started crying • I never pay much attention to expiration dates • I didn't expect to see a hawk perched on the chair of my dining room • My parrot liked me, I think, but it would never tell me anything useful • Lola never had a chance • The note from Kayla was a summons to the basement, a place which creeped me out, but it was Kayla, so I had to obey • The only time ol' Greg Nateson was going to wear a suit was at his funeral, which by the time I got to know him wasn't too far away • I poured the wine into the ocean • My gast has never been so flabbered as when my sister decided my husband was too irresistible to pass up • Dan was only 12 years old, but he was also the only person on the planet who could talk to the Genarians when they invaded the moon • Don't put me in the position of having to be responsible for you for even one second, let alone a year • The investigation determined that the day before Alfonso received the clock, a famous astronomer, who was also a golf enthusiast, had died • Despair, while justified, does no one any good • I was the only passenger who walked away from the plane, the rest of them mostly dead or dying • The dinner hall was a good three miles distance, which meant, given the meager helpings doled out by our masters, the work of getting to dinner took more calories than I would find there, so I elected, on that day, to go without • The following experiments are respectfully submitted to the committee as possible ways to understand our world • Alec stole so many library books he had to rent storage lockers to keep them all • Our lovemaking never amounted to anything much • My husband took to death with studied dignity and a sense of curiosity that infuriated me • Beauty in your child is both a gift and a curse • Ghost towns aren't so bad, once you get to know the ghosts • The thing about children is they are so dimwitted that they don't know their very existence messed up the order of things between two people • The taxi was a new model, the kind that floated above traffic, all lofty and superior like • My wife always got scared whenever she heard a siren • The heat in Calcutta is a physical thing • My daughter refused to go outside under any circumstances unless it was after sunset and before sunrise • Clyde Newman swung his ax through a chunk of wood he had set up on the chopping block behind his grandmother's house • There is only one story • You'll never see an animal, wild or domestic, choose to carry a wallet • The value of my body was never in question • The family wouldn't leave so we did what we had to do • My father called and said he needed to talk to me about his will • Don't grow up where you were born, just don't do it • The farm wasn't doing anyone any good • They moved into the house that had been for sale for over a year and were as sad and bedraggled as the house itself, maybe more • I noticed there were no umbrella shops in Phoenix, so, sensing an opportunity, I opened one, with hopes that I would get rich by forcing everyone who wanted an umbrella to come to me • The wolves • Sven stood watching the ocean liner coming in to dock and was having trouble reading the name on the bow • Everyone does paperwork, even the enlightened one • "Checkmate," said Randy as he moved his rook to the critical square, completing the trap he had prepared several moves ago, and put out his hand • One thing you never want to see on your doctor's face is a puzzled expression accompanied by a mystified "huh" • I had my money in real estate, on the advice of my mother • My friend Fiona never bought anything from any store ever • Beacon Rock was my path back to sanity • I like the idea of cutting off the hands of thieves • Listen, ghost, don't try to tell me you're my dead husband Cody when I know Cody isn't dead yet • The distress signal came from a sector of the galaxy that had been off limits to human craft for at least several centuries • Some towns seem tailor-made for people who are in witness protection • I was the one who started the whole thing, me, and no one else, despite what you've heard in the press • Her name was Nionc Tigo and you've most likely never heard of her • You can fault me for my prejudices, of which I got plenty, but if you need to track down someone, anyone, you need to know I got a 99.5 percent success rate in catching those that don't want to be caught and I lie awake at night fretting about that point five percent that gave me the slip • The blacksmith was burly, as befits someone of her profession • My husband was a lazy slob, something that was *not* apparent when I married him • Roger slapped his mittened hands together and squeezed his shoulders up to his ears • The one with the gun asked me who she should shoot first • The moon never keeps its secrets • The man who would soon be known as a terrorist removed his weapon from his coat pocket and pointed it at the man bearing a name tag indicating he should be addressed as Harvey K • The hummingbird fell out of the sky and rested on the sidewalk in front of Darryl's house, where he found it that evening • Faith called me up and said there was definite proof that the Second Coming had arrived and the new-born was now at the free clinic over on Sixth and Bellingham, receiving gifts and visitors, and would I come with her, please, to offer our respects? • Jean grew tired of her volunteer work—the homeless were always going to be homeless—and elected instead to watch TV and eat ice cream all day • The two of us held court in the neighborhood for many years, but it wasn't my choice, or my dog's, it just happened • I won't bore—or horrify—you with the details, but I survived the first night of the battle and hoped I didn't survive the second • I could tell she was old, but I could also tell she had been well taken care of, or had taken care of herself, and that it was important to her that she never miss a meal • If you have to go around telling people you're a genius, then most likely you aren't one • All he had to do was love me • Our crime was simple: we built bridges across the gulfs, we crossed those bridges into dimensions that were not our own, and we caused pain and death to entities that we encountered in those foreign dimensions • My only rule in life, if anyone ever asks, is to eat dessert first • My mother, a long haul truck driver, always used to say: "If you got it, a truck brought it" • I was at the Walmart politely haggling with the cashier over some prices when the manager came to me, flanked by two fat guards, and asked me to leave • I worked my ass off and I was still poor • When the aliens came, they stocked the oceans with their own fish and then they came with huge boats to harvest the next generation of alien fish and it was all so discouraging for us humans because there was nothing much we could do about it, and the worst part was that the alien fish displaced all of our fish and we couldn't eat the alien fish because it made us sicker than dogs • Shoplifting was a way of life that worked for me • When we got to the cottage, we found that the raccoons and bears had gotten to it first and had not cleaned up after themselves • Joana's stomach tightened as she saw the group huddled around a campfire, each with a mug in their hand • I was only eight when I knew my destiny • I feel sorry for horses, always have • My father was always less mature than me • Murder isn't entertainment • I'm a woman, but people still call me the tax *man* • I watched the Corbet Building collapse on TV early Sunday morning • The mice • What they did, which is wrong, is that they overlaid a grid on the park and divided it up into zones, as if the cougars and bears and snakes and so on had any inkling of what a zone is • Listen, ghosts like me, we need love too, just like anyone • Mummies scare me • He kept telling us he was Russian, like that mattered to any of us in the school yard as we prepared to pound him into the ground • Horses lie • I learned to move things with my thoughts • Don't talk to me about zombies unless you're ready to be one • Don't let the breeze rustle your feathers • My acupuncturist was a real prick • Beards just make a man look lazy • Some would say five ex-wives is a bit much, and being the guy with five ex-wives, I would have to agree with them • Maybe you think you know what's inside your skull • Bake me a cake, please • Some cities pick your pocket, others pick your brain, but they all pick you unless you want to hide, a strategy no one with any sense would recommend • When the time is right, I'm going to tell my wife all about what happened • The chickens made things difficult for everyone on the farm but it wasn't my fault • After I shot the elk I ate most of it right where it fell, fending off wolves and vultures the whole time • Children don't deserve the love we give them • Roxanne Parker has no time for children • I had the privilege of seeing my ship brought up from the ocean floor • The crash test dummy, it woke up in the middle of the crash, and I'm not kidding • First time I saw him, he was not the giant I came to know him as • The Count tasted of lavender and salt, like a flower cast upon the sea • My first jump and I had to share the booth with a man named Jerry who was also a first timer and way more nervous than me so I ended up being the one to comfort him, when, truly, I was a complete wreck myself and was more than half prepared to end up being smeared across the cosmos in an arc of misplaced atoms • Warren awoke with a feeling that he had somehow been reborn overnight, and it was not until he was halfway through his breakfast that he realized this day would be his last • Billie didn't think about his life much, but when he did it gave him a pain in his gut • Fifth grade, man, you gotta be ready for it or you'll be eaten alive and I'm not kidding • Einstein, after he fundamentally changed our concept of the universe, tried to invent a better refrigerator • I live alone on a mountain, but I ain't no guru • When the ore ran out, we started digging up beautiful women, a strange thing indeed, one which caused a great deal of consternation among some of the miners, and unbridled delight for the rest • In spring a young man's thoughts turn to matters of war • I will give civilization this much: it was fun while it lasted • The rabbit didn't know it was going to be my dinner that night • You don't so much hear a rattlesnake's rattle as you *feel* it, in your spine, a primal touch that leaves no doubt of the danger you are in • The lobby was packed with hippies • No one gots to tells me animals gots feelings, I already knows it • Ava Berger was immortal, and she was also what many would call, with admiration, a force of nature • Obituaries are silly things • I can go a few weeks, even a few months, without killing someone, but then the fever comes over me and there's only one way to cool it down • We fed the youth tales of glory, just so they would sign up for our obscene war • The silk threads cut deep • Adam's potato-leek soup was always an exercise in sublime beauty • The life of a mathematician doesn't add up • The fixer dragged the ghost out of the wall and laid it on the floor and smashed it flat, much to the astonishment of those assembled to hear it speak • The man on the bicycle was texting and didn't notice the kid in front of him on the sidewalk until it was too late • The virus had done something to the brains of the adults, so kids like me, we had to form gangs for self defense • Frontier jails usually aren't escape proof • Everyone's blood is the same color, more or less • Firefighters don't just die • The Pope was coming to town and the mayor informed me that His Holiness was going to wash and kiss *my* feet, if that was okay with me • Fairies commit murder, it's true, and not as rarely as you might think • The faculty gathering, boring from the start, had degenerated to pointless small and shop talk • Not sure what the critical mass is for my profession, but every town, once it gets to a certain size, it needs private investigators • Insensitive jerks are my weakness • They tell me I have a disease but addiction feels more like I'm a hostage than I have an illness • Leslie, the shyest, quietest kid in school, spends her time alone, painting pictures • I didn't want to kill the first one, but once I did, the rest were much easier • He was one of the little people, commonly labeled children, and he had a knack for disappearing, like a ghost that wants to kill you with fear • The bullet holes in the wall felt like a way to tell the winners from the losers • In the newsroom, if you had pictures of two bodies, one male and one female, you always *always* led the news with the dead female, no matter her age • My assignment was to review the latest symphony by a composer whose early work was incandescent with joy and enthusiasm, but whose later pieces were stately and plodding • Kafka didn't know what he was talking about • I was sure I had a happy childhood until I met Hans, who convinced me otherwise with impeccable logic and an unrelenting need to prove himself right • Thieves need to plan for retirement, just like anyone else • The comet, if you were of an open frame of mind, could remind you of a paintbrush, slapping white across the sky, making the milky way into some kind of graffito or mural • Borges was a blind dude • Phyllis stared at the man with unblinking eyes, matching him glare for glare • The headhunter didn't like his title but he liked me, a fact that troubled me more than flattered me • I was struggling, mightily, with the thought that I was now human • The robot thought it was self aware, but it was only fooling itself • Her hands looked like veterans of particularly brutal wars • The mountain range left bite marks on the sky • The kid had an attitude that was distinctly non-deferential to me, which I admired, but which I also had to crush out of him • The weather guy on TV said hurricane Cupid was not in a loving mood, and the darkly threatening sky outside my window seemed to confirm his pessimism, though I held out hope the storm's arrows were going to be soft things, and maybe launched with tiny arcs as well • Jennie knew about them • I *sensed* a spider in the house • Kaylee tries to ignore the lurch in her gut, which sometimes tells her something bad is coming, but usually just means she's nervous for no reason • The moon illuminated our faces in a disturbing way so we looked like ghouls about to perform some gruesome act • The theory of temporal uncertainty was first postulated early in the twentieth century in a short article by Ibaldo Umbra, an obscure Italian physicist who moonlighted as a fortune teller and palm reader • If you want to catch a rainbow, you have to be cunning about it, because rainbows are quick and they hate being trapped • Grandparents and grandchildren are often bonded together by their mutual fondness for sweets • You could say Bernadette was odd, but you would have to qualify that by saying she was odd in a very conventional way • Because of the chemo, the summer of 2014 turned out to be my last marathon • I started out poor and obscure and ended up rich and powerful just before the people I helped turned on me for good • My kid carved a devil out of wood • Experts come in many forms, thought Gayle Deeds, but the man standing in front of me is not one of them • The spirits were hungry for love • The blood-red sun soaked the parking lot in orange light • Ghosts don't need a reason to be • I heard the tornado before I saw it • I ran for county commissioner when I was six years old • Love is like a well: easy to fall into, but almost impossible to climb out of • Our family grew potatoes, tons of them, year after year after year • The new regime decided it was illegal for citizens to own land • God was having a really *good* day the day he made lotus blossoms • I showed my grief to the world by wearing black every day for a year, which broke my budget • Just before she rode the asteroid into the sun and left this reality, Cecilia said I should keep a diary of my life • People think prisons are part of the natural world and can't imagine a society without them • If I was a whale I have no doubt I'd have issues about the state of the ocean • No, the customer is absolutely *not* always right • My parrot didn't say anything, ever • Food stamps are a form of punishment and shame all rolled up into one potent slap in the face • My passengers were dead, every one of them, and so was I: a bus driver piloting a ghost vehicle through hell • Listen, I already had nine sisters, okay, so another baby in the house wasn't going to bother me at all • I never laid a hand on the kid, although I did whisper to him that it would be best if he stopped fighting and just took the blows from my buddies, a gang of bullies, who were determined to shut him up at any cost • The job turned out to be more than I had bargained for and clearly wasn't going to cover my costs, let alone the wear and tear on my psyche • In my family the rule was never to be sentimental about trees • I ran the company store and people detested me, but I was just as much a victim as the customers, believe me • The news came today: my doppelgänger had died • The Easter rabbit never had a name, which bothered me when I was a kid, and still seems unfair to this day • My French, being rusty from years of misuse, meant that the waiter brought me exactly what I didn't want • He was a beggar on the street, not a nasty one, but, still, he had no call to propose marriage to me, none at all • The star, now a hundred times brighter than it was the day before, became an object of much interest as well as more than a little suspicion • I was tracking a gang of railroad thieves across the eastern half of the Oregon Territory and found them one night, huddled around a campfire, easy pickings since I was carrying two loaded Winchesters and knew how to use them simultaneously • I was visiting my sister Rachelle and trying to understand why she had become hostile towards me when the sky cracked open and thick pink fluid streamed down from the heavens and splashed onto her backyard • Faber's training lasted three months, which seemed a waste of time and resources, considering he was being sent to the front lines and would probably survive a day or two at the most • A husband and wife both die at the same time • My mother, while she was birthing me, happened to be on the US-Mexican border, which meant I was born a US citizen, while she was still (partly) in Mexico • I spent the afternoon applying paint to a canvas, an activity that held no interest for me, but which I knew would bring me a substantial amount of money, a situation both absurd and gratifying • We went to France for a month but ended up staying 20 years before we realized we missed home • If you've never walked the ground in your bare feet you are not a true child of Earth • Rich people have always scared me • It takes Alice Forts a few minutes to understand her situation is not exactly dire, but not truly safe either • Raymond Montaigne's garden gave him much joy until it began producing mutant plants that no one had ever seen before • Harriet had just a few minutes to bring the children to something resembling safety • Money changes nothing • Games shouldn't matter, but they do, they matter a great deal • Sell everything, I told my best friend, and come live as a moon rat like me, down in the caves where sanity rules • The theater was simple, elegant, and overwhelmingly large • I don't remember exactly how old I was, but I do remember the man and what he did to me • I was the town's best Reiki practitioner for a short time • The lifeboat held my ex-husband, among others, which made me pause and consider how important it was to save myself • I could see some on the jury were sympathetic to my case, but, clearly, not enough of them • Word was getting around that Joel was a dream artist to avoid—he could give only unpleasant dream experiences • All happy families are imaginary • The bodies got uncovered completely by accident one morning in early June when Bea was in her garden weeding • He had the blank stare of a blind man, but I could tell he wasn't blind, which put me on high alert, calculating, as discreetly as possible, a quick escape route • Don't show me pictures of dead babies • The odor of cabbage, cooked to a soft and disgusting consistency, hung like a horror show vapor around my friend • The mermaid looked lost and broken in the net • My brother changed his name to Rick when he was in his 60s, which tended to alienate him from the family, a result he was hoping for and which I helped along as best I could • I always wondered if colors had a favorite color • My elementary school years were a rush of social engagements and deep learning • A leech had just burrowed into my right arm • When your father is the minister for the church everyone in town goes to, your life is pure hell • Road rage is dangerous, sure, but sometimes it's the best way to—no, never mind, there is no best associated with road rage • Randal was hugely green and as hopeful as photosynthesis allowed • I put my ear to the apple and listened to the seeds conversing with the worms • Find the devil, grab her by the lapels, and slap her across the face several times • The clouds were dark, but the truth was darker • I was built some years after the new codes were put into place, so the earthquake, despite its out-sized strength, didn't bother me a bit, even as my girders trembled and my windows rippled and my roof shimmied • The dust cloud came and never left • When he was young, the old man lived by the sea and spent his days at the shore, listening to the water lapping on the rocks • My aunt knew stuff no one else did • The weather rarely matched my mood, but that morning the pelting rain and grayish light, thrown down as if the gods were irritated with their creations, seemed to agree with my need to insult someone, and quickly, before the impulse dissipated • I've never inked a drunk person, at least knowingly, but I have inked people who I knew were going to regret their tattoos • The operator corrected me for mispronouncing my own name • In a large room, windowless and dark but for a small reading lamp illuminating the dry, crisp pages of an old book and casting a subdued glow that only penetrated the blackness a few feet, Pontos, a thin boy just touching adulthood, pulled a hand through his hair and rubbed the inside corners of his eyes • The temperature that Christmas eve crept up close to 90° Fahrenheit and this was, let me emphasize, in the *northern* hemisphere of planet Earth • Trak's senses were immediately alert, which happens when a person wakes up with a gun pointed at his face • "You'll have to let go," Vivian said hoarsely, "if you want to survive with any of your insides intact" • My father spent his last few weeks watching soap operas on the television mounted on the wall at the end of his hospital bed • My favorite thing to do, when I was new to town, was to take my umbrella out on sunny days just to soak in the looks I got and to tell passersby, as politely as I could, that, yes, they were right, I *was* crazy • I never did like frogs, so there was no way I was going to kiss one • If you are poor in this day and age, the only explanation possible is that you are stupid • A lot of people aren't aware of this, but murder is a profession with a professional code of conduct • The abacus revealed its secrets slowly • The ache in Victor's ear was unlike any ear-ache he could recall • Cheryl loved being a soldier, no matter which era she was deployed to • The newborns, all 13 of them, pressed on Gus's consciousness to such an extent that he seriously considered culling them to a more manageable half dozen or so • The coin was faded and covered with a greenish-blue blotchy kind of lichen, reminding Gwen of the star bursts she sometimes saw on rocks while hiking • I knew a guy who loved to tell the story of the axe that lasts forever • My sister was in jail for putting a dose of brain damage on the guy who gave me two black eyes after I wouldn't suck his dick after our date, but you know, life is like that and I told my sister through the glass at the prison visiting room that I love her more than ever, which made her cry like a baby, and me too, I know it's crazy, but me too • Look, I was perfectly happy slopping around in my little pond as a frog and I didn't need some wide-eyed lovesick blonde *princess* slobbering over me and turning me human, okay • My helmet didn't fit anymore • It wasn't until after Mark had moved to the Oregon coast that he learned it was nestled in the heart of the part of the continent that someone had dubbed Ecotopia • As Rex passed from one building to the next, lights dimmed in response to his presence, creating a kind of flowing night that felt more like an article of clothing than anything atmospheric • I've tried both sides of crime, the tribe of thieves and the tribe of law enforcement, and I'm still not sure which one suits me best • We turned the ocean into a garbage dump • The executioner displayed no empathy that day • My cat always turned her nose up at fish, but she loved bacon • One thing they don't tell you before you visit Costa Rica is the prevalence of their 5-inch cockroaches • Our county has, as one of its residents, a kind of red lizard that lives nowhere else in the world • Us kids were named Topaz, Quartz, Emerald, and Ruby because, as my mother put it, we were her jewels • The house clung precariously to a cliff, as though daring the Earth to dislodge it from its perch • The cowboy was green, and not from envy • Isabelle Langolier always thought of herself as extremely lucky • You gotta be seen and you gotta be lean and it doesn't hurt to be mean • First thing I noticed was that the elevator stopped at the 13th floor when there *wasn't* a 13th floor • My sister is, like, some kind of genius and the government is always asking her opinion about stuff that I don't know anything about and I don't mind telling you that totally *sucks* because she is way way stuck up about it • The gang of thieves I ran with when I was 14 was the best family I ever had • The island had one palm tree, like in all those cartoons, which made me laugh in a hollow, sad kind of way • My roommate had a way of removing taste from any dish she made, which is why, after a time, I began taking over her cooking nights, a turn of events that satisfied us both • I was a translator in those days, the kind who doesn't know his own culture and goes looking for meaning in foreign texts • The stars *made* copper, no argument, but it takes guys like me to *dig it out* of Earth's crust • Some of my friends consider my brother Jerry to be a genius, but I know better • God *damn* this blizzard • Marcia could read minds, but only of animals, not humans • No one heard officer Watson's last words • Two days before the murder, Ransom Dave drove high up into the mountains and held his breath, waiting for a sign from the heavens that would help him decide what he needed to do • If you're going to live on the moon, you need to really *mean* it • Death is the best disguise • Don't trim your nails around me, please • The village grew up beside the wall and moved with it over the course of centuries • I played my drums at the corner of Wilmot and Twelfth every afternoon for a year • Let me put it like this: love has issues • On her deathbed my wife made me promise to only remarry if my new wife was less beautiful than her • The tea was bitter, like my mood • Sunlight gave the fur a luxurious sheen, flecked with bits of saturated gold and points of luminous blue and Bernard felt he didn't deserve such opulence, not while people were begging in the street, but he wore it into the city anyway, resolving to give the first beggar he saw a nice new twenty dollar bill • I couldn't believe Trey actually dared to come to the prom after what he did to my best friend Gene • The dock was composed of rotting wood • My cell is spacious enough • Children understand war • The creek was cold from snow melt • I was surrounded by cops ready to kill • My drinking days included many nights of debauchery, but my daughter already knew that, or should • Night, infernal night, returned with an attitude • It wasn't Gloria's idea to break into the grocery store that night, but it was her expertise that kept us from getting caught • Chuck's puppets bugged the hell out of him • Twice upon a time I lived happily ever after • I used to be made of porcelain, which meant I could easily shatter, but ever since the permanent fog came, I've been made of flesh, a substance, I've come to believe, that's even more fragile • Before I put my chain saw blade to the tree, it had a few things to say to me in its photosynthetic leafy accent • When we played cowboys and Indians as kids, our favorite phrase was "It's just a flesh wound," but our favorite action was dying messily and over-dramatically • The dirt was fluorescent • I had a donkey I didn't know what to do with • The city woke from its slumber with a ferocious yawn that tore off roofs and sent people sprawling onto the ground • I own several laundromats here in my medium-sized town and I spend my days maintaining them and keeping the competition from gaining a foothold, but it's a full time job and lately I've been slipping, so that my livelihood is at some risk of disappearing, which explains, I suppose, my current dark thoughts, centered as they are on acquiring sufficient fire power in the form of guns to discourage any more incursion into what is rightfully mine • We talked to insects in those days • God handed me a pocket knife—he said he never went anywhere without it and it sure was a nice one with about 14 different blades and scissors, tweezers, pliers, a couple of screwdrivers, all kinds of stuff—and He said "Make a notch at the base of your thumbnail" • Earnest Everet Sanders got rich much later than was normal in polite society • I did crimes, a lot of them, but I never hurt anyone except that one time at the gas station, which was an accident, I swear, but still • The water was not what I expected • The argument was a trivial bone, but we gnawed on it—sometimes taking turns, sometimes clashing teeth—for the rest of the evening and into the next day • The animals, especially the smart ones, want to believe in our goodness, I think, but they are stopped by our behavior again and again • I learned to hypnotize people when I was quite elderly, but refrained from putting my knowledge into practice until it was a matter of life and death • The magic candles were faulty • Nothing exquisite about a corpse, so I don't know what those surrealists were going on about • I never used to believe in zombies • My memory of the hole in space is sketchy, at best • The bandits shot one of the tellers as a warning to us that they were going to be serious about shooting any posse that followed them across the desert • When I was about 12 I met a woman at the local public library who was in her 70s and who talked about a country she had visited where dead folks gathered and complained about the weather • People you know are more mysterious than people you don't • Blind people, I can't help this, always make me feel guilty because I can see flowers and they can't • My bruise was the color of ink • The dolls all woke up at the same time • Harriet played tennis most of her life, and for the duration intended to lead a cheerful life • Beauty trumps everything else, except maybe illness • Bruno handed me the report—all 695 pages of it—and told me I needed to have a concise and accurate two-page summary of it on his desk first thing Monday morning • The bomb was a beautiful thing, as awful as that sounds • Curtis opened his doors on the 31st day of his fast • One summer I played a gunslinger in an Old West show at an amusement park that offered very little of an amusing nature to anyone • You take Interstate 84 out of Portland, Oregon, going east, and you'll get to my town, though you might just want to skip by it • The snake had a wide smile • The fool left tracks in the snow that were easy to follow and follow them I did • I heard violent snuffling sounds outside the tent • In my experience, waves thrown up by hurricanes are the best ones for surfing • My gifts are few and sub par • On the banks of the Colorado River a thin young child named Edgar found tiny shells, some plastic waste, a discarded shoe, and a corpse • Samuel Havelstom always visited the fortune teller before going to the doctor • It's a disconcerting thing, to say the least, to have to hunt down your own clone • Brooke hoisted the chainsaw up to waist level and prepared to bring down the hundreds-year-old fir • STDs are the ultimate finger wagging in your face telling you how naughty you were • The town had no hearing residents, and I did not know how to sign • I was the one who discovered the president was a werewolf • Dogs are basically wild and I'm not, hence the high fear factor • The church had a wedding and a funeral on the same day and I was at both • The rustle of starchy lab coats always put Brenda at her ease • Our first anniversary was a somber affair • Robin ingested food like a tornado consuming wooden houses • Ben and Hope don't fall in love, but they get married anyway, mostly because they are both terminal • The note was too high • We loved each other for quite a while, then things changed • You couldn't sleep, even for a few seconds, if you wanted to stay alive • Street people, when I was one, would share food with other street people, even if it meant going hungry • An overcast May morning • People say a lot of things about Will that aren't true, most of them very complimentary • Five people in my family have killed at least one human being • My face never betrays my emotions • Even though I'm retired, lots of people still come to me for tattoos because, well, I don't like to say it, but I'm really really good at it and my tattoos, they have something about them, something people call magic and I call crazy • The first thing Mae noticed was the green slime hanging from the door into the lecture hall, a sure sign that the professor was an alien • It's not my fault I was born a dragon • I asked the librarian why do we even have libraries anymore when I can access the whole world's knowledge from my smart phone? • I usually live and let live but there was something *wrong* about the hoop pinned to the checker's nose

and even though I knew I shouldn't, I told her how ugly it looked •
They called him The Dentist when it leaked out that he collected
the teeth of his victims • Trade my legs for wheels, please • In the
summer of my tenth year I stowed away on a ship headed for Tri-
ton • Bus travel sucks • Beth didn't look good that morning • They
wanted my money and were only too happy to cause me injury if
that's what it took to get it • I started crying, shedding tears like a
river, and I didn't stop until my town was flooded • Fay's feet executed dance steps she herself could not follow • When I first met
Holly, she was trying to be incognito and I only knew her from the
magazine covers, but I saw through her disguise pretty easily and
she hated me for that • The mountain lion followed me to school
every day for a month • I got nothing against centaurs, I just don't
want to be married to one • All happy gangs are alike, but all
fucked-up gangs are each dysfunctional in their own unique way •
You put a fish hook through your finger, you got no one to blame
but yourself • I said it way back before anyone else and I'll keep
saying it because it's the truth: cattle ruined the West • Melville
Bryant will never tell you what happened to him • My daughters
were fighting again, and, to my shame, I did not stop them mostly
because I found their antics in this vein to be sublimely entertaining • The saloon held three rustlers, two bank robbers, a couple of

railroad saboteurs, and at least one counterfeiter, but the sheriff ignored all of them in favor of the woman in the corner, drinking by herself, who was a dead ringer for the assassin who had shot his deputy in Laramie last month • The clothesline marked the perimeter of our position, but the tool shed next to it, obscuring our line of sight, made it a difficult position to hold • The pelicans • The duct tape was tight and hard against my lips • Sophia eats snot and I know it's true because I saw her • It was just me and the growling dog and I was pretty sure who was going to win • Never tell your secrets to a writer • Someone named T. Hoppen sent me a package in the mail the size of a Rubik's Cube but I didn't open it for 50 years • During the flood, Mel couldn't get his medicine • Forensic science is a joke • Dead end streets are my favorite kind • The hardest part about dying was figuring out what to do next • Once the lights go out, my head explodes • Agent Mandie Rock assassinated the president to save the country—and her son • Listen, it's just not true what they say about kids and cartoons • Sandy hated living alone • "It's rarely a good idea," said the professor, "to open a story with dialog, even attributed dialog" • That was the year the dandelions invaded everything • The meeting was actually a trial in disguise • The apartment, with its low ceiling, close walls, and sparse furniture, perfectly captured Leslie's mood of desolation and she wasn't going to disturb the room or the apartment for at least a few weeks • The exterminator had yellowing teeth • My years as a monk were marked by boredom, serenity, joy, and terror • The murder plague hit our county on a normal spring morning • Religion always gets people right where it counts—in the heart and in the wallet • Once my husband was out of the way, me and my children could live in something resembling normal and safe • Sure, I'm a manticore, but that's none of your concern and doesn't affect the truth of what I'm about to tell you • The moon that night reminded me of a surveillance camera, tracking my every move • This sentence is self aware, and so am I • Words change over the years, trying on different shades of meaning like someone trying on different pants before deciding which pair to buy • The robots turned to eating fruit in their final days • In our family we all hunted except for me • I had celebrity status, but I didn't know how to use it without pissing people off • I got that feeling you get when the car behind you inexplicably follows your every move, turn for turn, lane change for lane change, for a lot longer than feels com-fortable • We kept the monster quiet for as long as we could, but as she grew from infancy to adulthood, she began to assert her right to be heard • Honey sticks to everything • Spend a day in family court and you don't need anything else in the form of entertainment • I knew what happened, and I knew the consequences of denying reality • There are no good slaughterhouse jobs • According to my mom, spiders in our house, even though they *totally* creep me out, are a protected species and I better not forget it • Green is no color for cowards • I awoke very early and decided this was the day I was going to give my child away • I ran a school for burglars • At 15, nothing much should scare you, but I was petrified of meteors, thinking one was going to fall on me at any second and knowing there was nothing I could do about it • I didn't know what the soap was made of, and some instinct informed me that I should not investigate the matter, lest I become horrified by the facts of the world • I had a career until the pukes took it away from me • My aunt remarried after her husband died and everyone in the family was mad about it because she had lots of money and now it was all going to go to her new young groom • Whenever I see a rock by a body of water I have to throw it in just to see the splash • The wall over the seat on the subway showed a stark image of Fusil Empathy, but I didn't pay attention because I hated the name and hated his music even more • I found the table at a thrift store and brought it home, completely unaware that it was going to start talking to me • We don't know the first thing about stars, how they feel, what they think, or why they love us • The sun grew green wings just before it sailed out of view, leaving us in the dark • We found disgusting things under the carpet • The flowers cried for me • There's bears all around us all the time but we don't see them and that's maybe because they don't want to *be* seen • Petulia's column ran three times a week for forty years and no one ever knew she channelled the text from an ancient entity she had picked up on her trip to South America when she was just 23 years old • The stagecoach arrived two hours early, careening wildly off the prairie, pulled by frantic horses, and missing a driver • I tried out for football, who knows why, and was rewarded with a split lip and a bruised face • Some days just *work* • The quilt had a checkered past • My brothers were being obnoxious at the dinner table • Caroline's whistle brought a cab to a stop next to her on the curb, but the occupant of the back seat, a green clawed giant lobster, prompted her to wave the cab on • I had the body for war, no question, but the will wasn't there, and I spent the years I should have been in battle tending to the wounded instead, which led to my numerous attempts at suicide • Flatland was my neighborhood • The temperature had dropped way below zero and ice coated everything when the power blinked off • The bartender's hands reminded Gwen of a corpse's hands, pale and wrinkled and repulsive • They said they found a previously unknown creature, so they called me, an old retired Bigfoot hunter, to come look at the thing and I agreed to do so, much to my eventual regret • The pilot divided up the dead passengers after the crash according to weight, gender, age, and taste • I didn't know who Mortimer was, and did not care, until he walked into my house with a large package that looked more than a little suspicious to me • The snipers were bad enough, holed up in the hills overlooking town, but the worst part of that year was the cars, strewn like rat carcasses, derelict and broken, overturned and burned out, constant reminders of our loss of freedom • Some folks like to watch millionaires throw a ball • The war interrupted everything • My story begins in Montreal, not because I was born there, but because that's where my father died, which meant it was where I became the head of the household • Unicorns are assholes • There's nothing wrong with nostalgia if you keep it to yourself • Dreams will cripple you faster than anything • The memories weren't mine, I was sure of that • The neon sign alternated between red and blue, displaying the name of a beer that Mr Griffin had given up years ago, but which still persisted in creeping into his thoughts • Sometimes you just have to shoot your dog • Most of the time, there's no reason to doubt your eyes • Always respect a man's socks • My husband never liked my beard even though I always considered it my best feature • Comedy clubs were my pharmacy • When I was incarcerated I missed a decent haircut more than anything else • A fight is just nature's way of telling you you're alive • I will fat-shame every chance I get • Hate all forms of transportation • Both the gravediggers, Helmut and Raj, spit on the headstone and didn't bother to wipe their mouths afterward • If you go by raw numbers of dead and wounded, Hiroshima and Nagasaki were not as bad as the sustained firebombing of Tokyo which occurred in the month before the atom bombs dropped • I promised my mother I would go to Hell, if necessary, to secure her future • My Mom got torn into pieces by the monster but she's okay now, mostly • Cam knew, from personal experience, that not all deaths are marked by sadness or tragedy • My cape had magical powers but I was too polite to use them • I taught school for many years but had to stop when the kids started to irritate me, which was about the same time I started drinking • Back when things were tolerable, I had a dog that never got tired no matter how hard I worked him • The borders of my country exist on some sort of odd alternate reality which has never been fully described or understood, but which means my country is not on any map anywhere • Estelle was laid off from her bank teller's job and found employment in the local pharmacy, where she wore a crisp tunic, all white, and tried to answer customers' questions about medications and often got it all wrong, much to the detriment of the customers • My mother always took two weeks out of the summer to go live alone in a cabin by the sea and I was 12 years old before I found out that not everyone's mother did that sort of thing • I like the idea of naming babies by lottery • The unholy shit storm at the state department was not my circus • After the death of the world, a taco cart seemed like the appropriate response • The moon became my sanctuary • Doris had the money, and she paid the rent, which meant that when she died, I had to leave the house, which broke my heart way more than the fact of Doris's demise ever could • Looking through microfilm reels always gave me motion sickness • I was the driver that day, something I never got over and never will • I'm a kid, like, only ten years old, but you should still listen to what I say because it's completely awesome • In our group no one *ever* wears purple, so when Betty showed up sporting a fluorescent purple hat none of us could decide whether we should jeer her epic fashion fail or applaud her innovative spirit • We were supposed to hate the aliens, I know, but I never did • The cats • I was hidden behind trees when Scrat Cranston, easy on his horse, drifted into view and I raised my rifle and took aim at his chest, right about where his heart, if he had one, should have been • I was the corrections editor at *The Hollenberry County Gazette* and you can get a hint of the quality of their journalism by the fact that I made quite a bit of overtime money during my three years of employment there • The boys stared at us in a way that made it plain they didn't see us • Sleep is not so much a little death as it is a chance to commune with the true nature of life • Just as I would never extinguish a dream, I would never douse a flame, any flame, anywhere • The team that took down the Commander included a kid who claimed clairvoyance, an octogenarian with an eidetic memory, a laborer from Indonesia with a strong back, and three fashion models who knew weaknesses of the military that no one else knew • My pet alligator came back from the dead, jaws snapping, up through the toilet while I was sitting on it • We sat down with a road atlas and planned our trip from Florida to Alaska, with stops in the wastelands of Nebraska, Arizona, and Oregon, because, well, we wanted to see what the end of the world looked like, just for old time's sake • Dead deputies littered the landscape • I wasn't about to save anyone • The robots were uncomfortably close to one another • After hats went out of style—practically overnight, while I wasn't paying attention—I tried selling scarves, but there wasn't much market for those, either • The wolf was not exactly a pet, but also not exactly wild, especially the way it came and sat in our backyard, practically begging us to pet him, which we never did, except once • Snakes have legs, they just don't know it •When the check arrived at the table no one reached for it, or gave it any notice, until Briley cleared her throat and asked in a low tone if we were all agreeable to walking out of the restaurant without paying • The invaders were polite, at least, I'll give them that • I was made in the USA • Salma's methods were unorthodox, but they got results • Charles Darwin, the most capable and sought after detective in rural England, had a theory of the crime that evolved over the course of three very odd months of collecting evidence • It's just my wheelchair, nothing more • "You will find it to your benefit to do as I say from now on," said my partner • Another day, after so many before it, just seemed redundant • He had a dancer's body, trim and muscular, but then so did all of the guys at the audition • No one liked the family that lived on the edge of town • Love endures, no doubt about it, but it also morphs along the way into something quite different from what it was when it started • Avoid Oklahoma City at all costs • Don't get me started on dog owners • A breakup by texting is the lowest of the low, you have to admit • I was making a passable living by translating Japanese erotica into Swedish • It was not my life's ambition to end up behind a bar slinging booze for sad executives but you do something for a while and it ends up feeling like what you were meant to do • I made it a point to always use the

27th letter of the alphabet • I will remain anonymous throughout this book as way of protecting myself, my family, and my planet • I was collateral damage, a fact which saved my life, though it was a life, by then, that hardly seemed worth saving • We should all eat more dill pickles • Her lips were the color of blood • Larry's fashion sense was his sixth • I used the word tarry in its proper context and I got such a look from everyone at the party that I felt my face turn red and I wanted to leap into the punch bowl • Convert your body and mind into its digital representation and store yourself in a black hole • My uncle Tomas never travelled anywhere until the accident, when he lost the use of both of his legs • The gun's handle was slick with blood—I wasn't sure whose—but I was determined to hold it steady on one of the surviving invaders despite the darkness and the crazy mad beating of my heart • I was there the year the animals woke up and took over everything • I hate cleaning • I once held the world record for crying: seven years and three months without a break • The grass was restless again • My credit card had me for lunch every day • In my experience, reading *Don Quixote* when you're a kid will only turn you into a burden on your friends and family • The vine was thick and covered with sticky sap • My Dad didn't want me, but my mother died and he had no choice but to take me in • The tree took several nights to climb •

Biology taught me at least one big lesson: everyone is a chimera •
Birds in cages know exactly how the world works and who has the
power • I told my doctor, for the sake of my future bloodsucking
children, to make me impervious to garlic, crosses, and daylight •
They came in the night, figures with hoods, and tore Gabrielle's son
from her arms, and kept him for the next 15 years, returning him
to her only when he had served his purpose and was no longer useful to the regime • The morning stage brought the new school
teacher, a little slip of a woman, who was not going to survive a
Wyoming winter, let alone a school full of wild west kids • Sometimes, on special days, the weather will work a certain magic, and
everything suddenly becomes so clear that you think you can read
by shadow • The aliens had some decidedly unorthodox burial
practices • My dreams are all about being immersed in water •
Herman tries to fire me again, but he knows and I know that no
one else will work for him, so we have a truce in which I get a night
off and he has to sling drinks himself • First my fertility clinic went
bankrupt, then my matchmaking service barely got off the ground,
so then I stared a mortuary because, like my father told me, no one
has to get married and not everyone wants kids, but we all gotta
die, you know? • No one wanted to see this much rain in such a
short time • When her city came under siege, Holly learned to use

her magic in ways she had never thought possible • Denise had certainly seen her fair share of death threats during her years as state representative, but this one, delivered by hand, felt different • Again with the chickens and I have no words • Lou Pine was fast, no question, but he was no match for the plodding Tort Huss • The cage was made of candy canes • I was writing the lede to the front page story when the attackers stormed into the newsroom spraying bullets and blood everywhere • Back then if you wanted to get out of serving your country as cannon fodder, all you had to do was become a friend with someone on the draft board, and by *friend*, I mean offer them a bribe • For funeral day that year, like every year, I had my knife in a sheath strapped to my leg • I was climbing the building, just getting started, when I crossed over that invisible line that separates an injurious fall from a fatal one • I told my husband I didn't want to live anywhere near water • It wasn't until the fourth bullet went right through me that I realized the first one had already killed me and that I was now a ghost • My petition for reactivating my soul was denied • The statue in the square looked just like my grandfather • I decided that some soldiers shouldn't come home • I appeared before the committee, not because I was summoned, but because I deduced that eventually I *would* be summoned and elected to face them before all the evidence of my misdeeds came to light • You want a happy life, don't ever get caught alone in a room with a dead body • After seeing so many bright explosions, I suffered from post chromatic stress disorder for many years • Sometimes names mold themselves to the people they are attached to, and sometimes people mold themselves to their names • Can we start now? • Beulah's house smelled of sulfur, which prompted several in town to think of her as devilish, but that wasn't so • The milk had turned, but Seth, in a gambling mood, put some in his morning coffee anyway • Sometimes you're good at stuff you don't care about and really terrible at things you want to be the best at • My stigmata got infected • It is shockingly easy to convince people that other people need killing • Tegan held his cat's head in his hands and wondered what it would take, how much force would be necessary, for him to crush that little skull • All of the eggs in that dozen had double yolks • Never trust a grave robber • People used to have these things called *jobs*, or so my grandmother told me • Henrietta developed a logo for her activities and left it carved into wooden surfaces at her crime scenes • Sand really bugs me • We had a company store, and that's all you really need to know about our town • The cake leaned precariously to one side • His blood was not as red as it should have been • Jeremy Worcester, who had been told he had only a few days to live, sat in front of his Genie word processor composing his will • I hung a skeleton (human, of course) from the ceiling of the hallway, but after a few years I wondered if that was a truly wise thing to be doing • My father used to say babies were a drain on the economy and that the age people can legally get jobs so they could begin pulling their weight should be dropped to four years old, and I was never really sure if he was kidding or not • My uncle Latty sent me a letter in which he complained that his cell phone service had been cut off and asked if he could crash at my place for a few days, just until he got his act together and then he would be out the door for good, promise promise promise • The bar had the feel of a bomb that had been neutralized by experts • Antonio never felt more alive than when he walked in a graveyard • The keyboard had a sticky wwwwwwwwwww • We were a planet of fools • Jolisa never went into the part of town where the aliens from the stars had moved in until she lost her dog Foster • Many people will advise you not to get a tattoo and they are usually right • Cooking for one was sad enough but cooking for 100 was much harder on my emotions, especially since I wasn't very good at cooking anything and really had no wish to learn • My town is not on any map and my fellow citizens like it that way • One thing I always tell my students is that pleasing me is not the point of their education, at least not completely • The truly free person is destined to die young, or, at the very least, broken • I dug the trench behind the condemned so that when they were shot they would obligingly fall in, thereby making things a lot easier for me as far as burial was concerned • The parents did not care for their children, that was chillingly clear • We were living in an era when I actually had to take the time to explain to people why bigotry was a bad thing • Most people don't think they'll ever be a ghost • I smart man see tings no one see but only me • The garden had its points, but in the end there was no reason to keep it and I plowed it under to demonstrate my devotion to the purity of the land • I lost my wedding ring while I was weeding the garden and have looked for it every season since, a span of time during which my children grew up, my husband died, I stopped driving at night, and I got tired of weeding the garden • I pulled the bowl off the shelf and turned it over and saw my name——Orville—printed on the bottom in a script I vaguely recognized as similar to my handwriting when I was 11 years old • My last words will be some combination of pithy, memorable, appalling, uplifting, and disgusting, and will be spoken in perfect and clear English in the company of at least two reliable witnesses • Origin stories are usually disappointing • Never liked putting people in jail, even really bad ones, so I began an amnesty program, which the good people of Glory did not take to and which accounts for my being an unemployed sheriff • Only an idiot sides with humanity against their family • The world is a load of shit, innit? • I concealed my movements through Seattle as best I could • My portrait of the queen was not nearly as flattering as she thought it was • "I'm not a magician," I told the client • There's a woman here who says she's my wife, which is crazy because I'm a woman myself, and there's no way I was a lesbian, I mean, come on, no matter how crazy I am now, living in this nuthouse, there's just no way • A voyage around the world on a sailing ship is no picnic, let me tell you • I'm an old lady but I don't have any cats, so put away your preconceptions and come look at my collection of shrunken heads • I got sympathy for victims, don't get me wrong, but you stay in the house with an abuser, that's on you, and I'm speaking from experience here, both as a someone who hit and someone who got hit • When I finally achieved a measure of wealth, I understood the contempt that a certain type of rich person harbors for everyone else • Marc envied his neighbors because they never seemed to care about anything • My dad named all his cars: Betty, Old Gertie, Matilda, Henrietta, and Ethel • The dead man held my interest for about 15 seconds • Henry stood on the St Johns bridge over the Willamette River building up the nerve necessary to drop into the water below, but he had second thoughts about his plan, and wished his wife was still alive so he could ask her the best thing to do with his grief • She was a giant that didn't live on a mountain and never wanted to • My night in Kamloops, British Columbia, lasted at least a week • I cut hair, but that's not who I am, not completely • I had fought in the streets of Galther City when I was a kid, so returning when I was 50 meant a major realignment of my memories and expectations and I wasn't prepared for it on any level • Ruth thrived in the age of mediocrity • When I turned 60 I stopped being kind; it was just too much work • Justin was born in a remote corner of Washington state, where the grass was dry, and creatures both large and small waited to be named • It takes some work, but if you put in the effort, you will see that everyone around you drags a dark shadow behind them • Kennedy never died of that gunshot wound, okay? • It ain't easy figgering the right thing to do when everything around you is fucked up to the max • I love my guns, all of them, every last one • This diary will never be read by anyone, I'll make sure of that • I knew the car was haunted by the way it smelled: hints of rotten fish with an overlay of peaches and vanilla • I never liked encountering teeth in my dreams • No one believed Gordie's story • Geras and Sebon travelled for several days, molding their bodies to the wrinkles of space-time, before they came to the rip in the universe • You'd think a war would keep the country enthralled, but people still found time to rob and murder, and I still had to be the one to find the bodies and make things right • He didn't know what a birthday was, that's how screwed up he was • Breathe • "Never trust anyone," said my father, "not even me and maybe *especially* not me" • The skunk under our house held the whole family hostage • The moths • I was getting a jar of olives from the fridge when I thought what would happen to me if my son died and then I started weeping and could not stop • Taking out the trash is my job and I take it seriously • My Dad died before I was born, but he knew he was terminal and he left me a notebook which I have never opened and which scares me to this day • William Shakespeare surveyed the Boston harbor as his ship glided into a world he did not know and would come to detest • Before I put on a uniform and became a killer for my government, I had honed my skills as a freelancer, and, I have to say, I preferred my life as an illegal serial killer over my life as a paid soldier • The fire spread so fast that no one had time to get dressed and we were all in the streets in pajamas, T-shirts, raggedy underwear, or wearing nothing at all • You gotta be really really careful with magic spells, let me tell you • My shirt needed ironing, but, being philosophically opposed to crushing creases out of clothing, I chose to enter the public realms with all wrinkles intact • The original idea was that my son Bernie would take over the shop when I died but what with one thing and another, I decided I wasn't interested in dying, thank you very much, so I'm still here and Bernie's still waiting and every day, it seems, he comes to me and asks "How you feelin' Pa?" • When I lost my memory, there wasn't much in the world to tell me who I was • It was the sort of place that made you shudder, thinking about what sort of people would actually choose to live there • Eleanor's best meals were breakfast, but no one put on breakfast parties, so she tried to learn to make dinner better in order to attract the kind of people who could advance her path through life • Even after ten years, the work did not get any easier • Don't tell me about God, any of them • No one, old lady or not, lives in a shoe, so just get over that particular conceit and follow me along on the true story, the one that involves no shoes • I was created by a 3-D printer • The eclipse was beautiful, in its way, but it also caused the biggest traffic jam Salem had ever seen • My dog and my cat died on the same day • When he was a child, Eric did not have nightmares, or very many dreams of any kind • In Detroit the evil caught up with us and crippled any connection my daughter and I had managed to forge over the last three days of our trip to my ex-husband's memorial • There's no cold like Winnipeg cold and the people who live here want you to know it • My house was a deep vibrant pink, the kind you sometimes see inside of seashells • You'd think an app that made you invisible would be a sure fire bestseller, but you'd be wrong • The screen glowed green in Amelia's face • Nudity loses its potency when it becomes ubiquitous • We were friends, of a sort, but only because our spouses were best friends • We wrecked Denver • I was 14 years old when my mother lost her hair from the chemo and I shaved my head in solidarity, which my mother didn't care for, taking to screaming at me and eventually prompting me to google the phrase "inappropriate appropriation," which is what she accused me of • Nick was methodically searching the dresser drawers when the owner of the house opened the front door and paused, like he knew something was wrong • The body was difficult to identify when I first saw it owing to the fact that his dog loved him so much that she had taken to eating him, probably the same night he died • All my professional life I have been involved with vital issues concerning the living, and I am therefore unaccustomed to carrying out the wishes of the dead, especially the dead of a nearly forgotten era • Deanna's sentence was not long enough to be an undue burden, but not quite short enough to keep her from imprinting on prison culture and making it her own • I call myself AAA Legal Services for a reason, and it's not because I'm Adams, Andrews, and Ashley • The band of robbers meant us no harm, so they said, they just wanted a night's sleep and would we be so kind as to fix them a meal, and in the morning they would be gone and we would have our ranch to ourselves again • Julie's pet basilisk was accused of staring her neighbor's cat to death • No one believes me when I tell them my agent is a nice guy • Hunger erases everything else • I don't want to hear any more stories about The Tilt • Snow fell all morning and afternoon, sucking the noise out of the world • I have always trusted numbers • A lunch date has its pitfalls and trapdoors • My suicide was scheduled for that afternoon, but before all that could happen, Renaldo dropped by for a visit and I felt obligated to entertain him to such an extent that killing myself after he left just seemed like way too much work • My aunt told me to never take advice from old people, and most especially not from old people like her • I had no idea—none—where the stuff under my fingernails had come from • Da inglish, she wuz da hardest to learn for my mudder, even while all the time I teach her whut I know bout it • Wildfire smoke turns early morning sunlight into a cake-like confection of orangy-yellow sweetness with a corresponding sugary fragrance that shouldn't even be there, but is • Suppose you lived on a spaceship, and suppose this spaceship was going through the void, awash in a vacuum, its destination long since forgotten, its purpose a mystery to all on board • I had never slept with a student before, and she had never slept with a professor before, so we were both hesitant and trying to act like we were worldly when I was sure both of us were actually ready to back out of the arrangement and save ourselves from certain shame • In the heat of the day, the creosote tree gave off an odor reminiscent of car exhaust, which reminded Ned of the accident, which made him shake uncontrollably for several minutes until he could regain his equilibrium • God went on vacation and left me to universe-sit • Road trips can kill you dead • The timeship needed cabin boys and Flynn, being an orphan, was a perfect fit • A plot emerged as all the deaths were revealed to be connected • A city of aisles lined with layers of shelves stacked impossibly high • Cobwebs were my social network • The air was hot on my cheek, too hot for comfort • I spent my life lying and don't regret it one bit • Mary's beloved hills were marred by the recent fire, displaying wide swatches of blackened tree trunks folded into the stands of healthy green trees • The guy on the phone said my brother was in jail and I needed to come up with bail money fast if I didn't want him to spend the night locked up with murderers and rapists • The birds sang songs I didn't know • The Greeks were stupid • I have a nice house on the coast of British Columbia • We knew from the start that she would be the first to go, but it was still hard to take and I found myself resenting her attention to detail in making sure all her affairs were in perfect order, even the messy ones • The waiter thought he was being discreet, but I saw him spit into Mike's huevos rancheros and the worst thing about it all is that I didn't tell Mike and he cleaned his plate without ever knowing and I never felt any shame about the incident • I've known three murderers in my life and all three were what you would call nice guys who wouldn't hurt a fly • My house was made for all seasons except my season of grief • My shoes, without my knowledge, had been soundproofed • Money trumps decency, every time • When you're a rabbit, you got to watch for predators every second of every day, something I understand on a cellular level • I found three spiders in the house one evening • The snake startled me, then I killed it • Denny left his car in a parking space on the 1500 block of Broadway and walked the mile or so to Fremont Street, where he turned right and waited in front of the dog-grooming place for his contact to arrive • It was the sort of place that you couldn't tell which season it was unless you already knew • If you want to save the world, good luck • I was out of the tower getting breakfast when the planes hit, but I let people think I was killed when it collapsed • When I got to be in my mid forties, my ability to fly simply by flapping my arms began to fade • It got to the point where I couldn't hear the confessions of another sinner, mostly because I was way way worse than any of them • I have lived in this city since before my earliest memory • I didn't want to start this with the word bastard in the first sentence, but the muse sometimes does things that are socially inappropriate and you have to make a decision on the spot and sometimes it's an embarrassing thing and there's nothing you can do about it • This memoir of my sunset years should be called *The Old Man and His Pee* • The blade was so sharp I didn't even notice when it cut me, so clean and pure was the wound • The king wanted to build towers, lots of them, but I counseled him against such foolishness, arguing that there was not enough money in the treasury, which explains, in a way, my current predicament • It turned out the top of a mesa in New Mexico was not the ideal place to hide a body • Graves offer their own pleasures • My garden was so beautiful that it won an award • In prison I kept to myself, which led to a lot of demons careening off the walls of my skull • Some crimes announce them-selves with fanfare and others hide under a rock with the slimy things, daring you to turn over the rock and look at the horror • I decide to let my hair grow forever • The robbery went bad soon after my partner decided he wanted to kill someone because that was on his bucket list • I rode the Pony Express for five weeks and that gave me all kinds of respect for the horses • 'Tis antigravity preserved my soul • Light was everywhere, clouding perception with a stifling illumination • I had a pair of dice tattooed on my arm to give me luck • The woman flying a sign on my corner may have been homeless, but I doubted it • I liked washing windows • I returned from the battle minus two limbs and it will be up to you to help me get through life • When illumination returned to my world, I felt a bloody mass of clotted hair at the side of my head, and took note of the man I had killed, who lay next to me, soaking up the rays of the midday sun • I turned my house into a casino just to pay the rent • The Mango Incident, as it came to be known, ended when one of the instigators surrendered all his fruit to authorities and submitted to an intensive interrogation • The sound of the creek: a gurgling grammar of cascading water molecules • My sentence was about to end and its terminal period was me walking out of prison into chaos • My nickname when I was a kid was Fartsy • I did real magic for years • The factory where I was born was having trouble finding markets for its products and was about to be shut down • It was the burst of times, it was the jest of times • The store was enormous and it was rumored that it held at least one specimen of every possible retail item in existence • The guy on the bridge was threatening to jump and I pulled out my phone and began filming and I don't feel guilty or bad about it so don't even try to lay your morality on me, just don't • We found the house by the usual method, but we were too late • The baseballs that season, on order of the commissioner, were orange • The solar sails had become colonies of parasites and I had to take care of them • See the smoke, feel the heat • If you go from relationship to relationship, one after the other without a pause, you might want to consider it's not a choice you're making, but more a kind of acting out of some compulsions • The ships sailing into the harbor were not from our time • Any farmer will tell you it's not God that giveth and taketh, it's the soil • Sometimes Anala thought about the weights she used, how they must think her daft to be lifting and lowering them over and over again • My hat that day, after a long afternoon of picking my guitar, held a subway token, two mints, three one-dollar bills, several pennies, and a note which read: *get a job and stop cluttering up the sidewalk* • Christiana was too clever for her own good • No one wants to see a man cry • Bridgit was an odd child, everyone in the camp agreed • The sheep I was counting, all of them, looked at me and told me I was not going to get any sleep this night or any night and I was going to have to get used to dealing with all that time on my hands • They wouldn't take me for the war because they said I was too young • Youth insults us all • Introverts have it made • The delay was not insignificant, which meant our attempt at subduing the crowd was going to be harder, especially with the dictator about to give an important speech • Calculus was easy for me • Angels got wings, that we know • My analyst said she wanted to see my shadow but I didn't oblige her because I knew she wasn't a true believer • My mother taught me that a full day's fast once a week ensures a willingness to live well • The hotel had a cute name for every room • The last thing you want to find out about your parents is that they collaborated in the killing of another person and the fact that it happened before you were born doesn't make it any easier • The oranges came from my tree and they held the sweet warm juice of summer • My mother used to say I was born wearing hiking boots, and I guess she would know • The interrogator comes in every day and asks me questions • "Bite me," said the dog • His favorite phrase was "eat my shorts" • Pregnancy is a state of mind just as much as it is a state of body • The flag was tattered • The service animal was an alien • Uncle Kasper returned from Mars with stolen artifacts that he gave to me • Beatrice refused to take family photos that included dogs • The weather that day reminded Zane of a couple of fighting cats, lightning clawing the air and big furry clouds strangling each other •

Thing is, you want to be part of today's culture, you got to know who the celebrities are sleeping with, and there is no use arguing the fact • Metha was a student of the great ship that had risen out of the sea and beached itself on her island's shore • I didn't ask to be brought to the station • The vet had her suspicions, but I told her the cuts on my dog were an accident and after some hesitation she prescribed painkillers which I ended up using for myself to get through that day to the next day when I would inflict fresh wounds on my dog and look for another gullible vet because that's what it took for me to survive that summer and my dog was a piece of shit anyway • Milton's patent application was rejected because he was six years old and the patent office said no six-year-old can know anything about optimizing the landing gear of a passenger jet, no matter how professional the drawings were • The taste of cinnamon always made me ill • The eggs, all two thousand of them, glowed in the dark • It's always good to open a story with either a wedding or a funeral, because love and death, baby, that's what it's all about • We got married when we were both 11 years old • My former students still think they have the right to monopolize my time • Not every dog is a friend at all, much less a best friend • It took a while, but eventually I cared about Lucia more than I cared about myself, something she said I should think of as love • It was a gamble, sure, but I had myself frozen—before I died • We were in the 14th year of the conflict, a time when no one on either side thought it would ever end • Clothes proved to be my biggest problem • The wars that define us aren't necessarily the wars that wound us, or make heroes of us, or reveal us as cowards • I spent a long time composing the ransom note before I captured the hostage that would go with it • I was a street juggler for a few summers back when people liked that sort of thing and would toss a dollar or two in my hat every now and then • The ocean shore is made for broken hearts • There are any number of reasons to get an education, but on no account should curiosity about the world be one of them • Fagan's way of looking at things always confused his friends and confounded his enemies • My uncle, he learned me all the ways to kill a man good, but he showed me bad stuff too • Simon's father goes south every year to service the giant mirrors in the scorched USA, where Simon knows only crazy people live • The city didn't so much eat its young as it crushed them and left them writhing in the streets, hoping for a killing blow • Lindman swung a bat like a lumberjack swings an ax • I saved one of them from jumping in the river and I regretted it ever since because now he says I am responsible for his life so he has taken over half my house and eats most of my food and shits in my bathroom and I have half a mind to choke him to death and feed him to the river after all • Florence liked her shoes silent and off grid, thank you very much • I killed my twin, but it was in the womb, so I got away with it • I was one of those kids who could do higher math when I was four years old, but it didn't make me a better person or keep me from ending up where I am now • I gave up smoking until it got trendy again and I followed the crowd, which I always do, and decided my lungs didn't need to be quite so healthy as they had been • My pictures and no one else's • I knows English better than any English professor you want to name to me • Life is subject to entropy, just like everything else • A week before we started, we found a map of the country and spread it out on the kitchen table • He shouldn't have been out on the water, being unpracticed in the art of kayaking, especially on such a stormy day, and he got swamped, and panicked and drowned while people on shore yelled at him, trying to get him to straighten himself, trying to keep him from dying because after all, he was one of them, he was a human being, however foolish • My court-appointed lawyer was a piece of software • 94 days after the film *Horror* was released, people who saw it began experiencing frightening visions • Milan waited around the corner as long as he dared, back pressed against the rough bricks, listening to the approaching footsteps of at least three enemy soldiers, before he decided to run • The lawn mower, after 23 summers, was the closest thing I had to a good reliable friend • After my medical training was complete, I came to understand that death was not so much inevitable, as welcome • My dog was ugly • People who don't care about their appearance are braver than soldiers, certainly, maybe even braver than public speakers • I wanted to divorce my wife but she was terminal and I couldn't bring that much guilt upon me • Skin color shouldn't be as significant as it seems to be • Turns out you can, in actual reality, live in someone else's skin • My husband doesn't know I've been fired so every day for a month now, I've been leaving the house and driving in the direction of my former place of employment until I get out of sight of the house and then I turn toward the sea and after an hour or so I'm on the beach, where I spend the day walking along the surf, communing with the pelicans, seagulls, and sanderlings • Me and Luci, we decided to take the ultimate road trip: five days of non-stop driving, going nowhere fast • The rose was useless on its stem • Patricia, when she found out she was royalty, began wearing a crown, something all her friends found less than amusing • Actually, I am embarrassed to say this, but once I did eat yellow snow • In those days we didn't think the oceans would rise as far as they have • I found a shopping list in the back of the junk drawer from 12 years ago and took it to the store and bought every single item on it as a tribute to the foresight of Fiona, who had written it just a year before she died • The whale filled the boxcar • There once lived three kittens who were all sisters: a white one, a black one, and another who had patches of both black and white • Sheila didn't know when she would talk to the ocean again • My shop was off limits to Gilda, the nastiest woman in town, and also, awkwardly, my sister • My shirt bore stains I could not identify • One rule to confuse them all • Break a brick in two, then break one of those pieces in two, and you've got a nice weapon with sharp cutting edges that fits snugly in your hand ready to hurl at anyone who gives you an ounce of trouble • There's nothing more life affirming than a well-attended funeral, and nothing sadder than a lone casket pleading for respect in an empty viewing room • Hylon the Magician was always at the center of things, the true power behind the world • The gang chose their towns carefully, always on the look out for indifferent marshals and incompetent sheriffs and found themselves a little burg in the foothills of Wyoming that was ripe for the picking • People hate beggars with such a passion that we have to defend ourselves against their violent tendencies • Missing shadows, sure, that's a sign, but even more telling is when you meet someone with silent footsteps because then you *know* you're in their zone • Mary wasn't surprised the day her cat started talking to her • There was a tiny blue smudge buried in the skin at the base of Lorraine's thumbnail • Andy told me people are the only animals that need pillows • Time is on no one's side • The plane went down near Baffin Island on a stormy night when there was no chance of rescue • I drew the map from memory thereby making it useful only to the spirit realm • I was five years old and my mother wanted me to wear a Nixon mask for Halloween and I didn't know who Nixon was and I started crying because I wanted to be Wonder Woman and my mother let me cry myself out and then explained to me how Nixon was way scary and that convinced me, at least for a short time • In school, if you're paying attention, you'll see the hard workers get nothing, while the brown-nosers get everything • One afternoon, not having anything better to do, I counted all my online accounts and figured out I had 258 different passwords and *I knew every single one of them by heart* • Henry woke up about 4 a.m. to the sound of the toilet bubbling ominously • Memory was a substance to him now • The cats came after me in a coordinated attack • The odor of dead creatures was, for many years, something I savored • Mother Earth's dance card wasn't full yet • Death beds should not be solemn, but they inevitably are • Harriet never trusted anyone, certainly not strangers • After my father was murdered I went underground and remained undetected for many years • Gabe's walk took longer than he expected • We called them multiple guess exams • Marriage was interfering with my love life • The cushion held secrets • Her laughter reminded me of whipped cream on strawberries but I never had the courage to tell her • I never thought I'd become a cultural icon • When Tee saw the new one named Mac, he knew right off that he wasn't a robot • Work hard, play hard, love well, remain active and alert, and don't mess with the natural order of things • One thing I've noticed about movies is that people will love them, even if they are bad • The play, by then in its fourth act, had me nodding off and snoring, much to the distress of Gayle, who had to elbow me hard at least twice before the gun, which had been brandished with no finesse in the first act, finally went off, felling the lead actor before it popped, and eliciting several startled cries from the audience, which were more engaging than the lackluster activity taking place on the stage • You could say I was a bad guy and I would not argue with you • My marriage wasn't arranged, but my divorce was, much to my objection • Coyotes are so smug • See the sky • Fried bananas, that's all I have to say • The alien plant, in its dried state, emitted a symphony of beguiling sounds, like a ghost humming an aria • The guy polishing my shoes looked to be at least 90 years old • I never wanted to run a hotel, but fate had other ideas • The nursery gave off an air of something undetectable and perhaps sinister, but definitely not cheerful • The famine was *not* a blessing in disguise, so don't tell me that if you want me to remain cordial • The raccoons in our neighborhood were numerous, bold, and vicious • I haven't seen a lot of dead bodies, so finding one on my doorstep was simultaneously frightening and fascinating • A baby's skull comes in pieces that move around like continents: calcium tectonics • Super hero comics never interested me • Halfway across the desert we pooled our meager provisions, calculated what we needed to survive for the next three weeks, and determined that at least one or two of us would likely perish before we reached the oasis • Vern sits by the portal, waiting for the next dead soldier • I never wanted to grow old • I was never hampered by excessive modesty • Why did dying take so long? • Annabel Annabel Annabel • The genie offered me three wishes, which was fine, I guess, but I explained to him that three just didn't cover my needs, not completely • My socks were covered with seed pods • Felicity spent way more time at the aft view port, drawing the stars, than her parents thought was good for her • When I first held your hand I remember you wanted me to back away and keep the personal space around you with nothing to mar its purity • The bow was multicolored and held Hazel's red hair in a soft bun that cascaded down the back of her head to touch her collar softly • I packed a rock in the snowball and threw it at my friend, which, I guess you would have to concede, made me a first class jerk • Cockroaches are misunderstood • Claire climbed all the super tall buildings in her city, evading authorities at every turn, then decided she would retire and write her memoir • The alien had many lives and many forms • Sometimes the undertaker interrupted my dreams • Stamp collecting is for fools like me • You want to do your kids a favor, arrange to die before your drooling and diaper years • I lived well past a hundred, a completely ridiculous age which my children were not prepared to deal with and which prompted a certain amount of contempt from them, for which, I hasten to add, I ascribe no blame • The policeman should not have had a beard, half-constructed or not • I never should have agreed to be best man, since I couldn't stand the bride • The ice was a nuisance • The dime novels made me into a hero, which I never had been • The spider entered the room with me and kept going, like it had an important appointment that it couldn't miss • The limo's tires all went flat at the same time, just as the president asked me what was wrong • In armed conflict, the important preliminary task for the warrior is to disappear • Surgeons are in a very good position to cover up their murders • On the night that Karm Nordja's world began to turn upside down, there was no one waiting at home • I was born in the year of the rabbit, but my heart has always beat for horses and always will • Beer never attracted me • Pain is an illusion and broken hearts is just a metaphor • I had to break the doll into three pieces • I named my tumors • The two figures off in the distance were armed, that was clear to Flora, and they were advancing on her house with what looked like determined resolve • My ex-wife said I should put flowers at the grave of the woman who donated her heart to me • When me and my sister were just kids, a child molester moved into the house down the street, only we didn't know it and neither did our parents, and he became friends of the family until we found out what he had done and then it was ugly what we did to him • The neck, harboring muscle, ligaments, tissue, channels, pipes, nerves, bones, and passageways, contains a lot of conduits • Serena often thought being a kid on a starship was about the most boring thing in the universe, except for maybe listening to her parents tell her about how great it was to be on a starship because they were saving humanity by finding another world where they could all live in peace blah blah blah • Tight-lipped and immaculately clean, that's how I remember him that first time he came to see me • If you know how many foster parents you've had, you haven't been in the system long enough •

You should never eat vegetables • No one knows, except me, what killed Mrs Worthington • I built a bird house in my backyard, but no birds ever moved in • The dance spilled out of the hall and into the streets where the rain, coming down pretty hard, served to refresh the dancers rather than dampen their spirits • I spent hours watching the chickens scratch at the ground around my house • The hawk skimmed the grass in the distance, then turned sharply in the air, acrobatic like, and I whispered a short prayer for the soul of the mouse that was about to be a meal • It's always disappointing to have a fool for a son • The mother-to-be lived in a poor neighborhood of the city • The house was affordable because it was located right next to train tracks on one side, and a graveyard on the other • You should never meet your heroes, true, but it is also best to never meet any of your fans • Artie gave away all his money before he died • You might never know if a man is a threat or a friend • The one thing Amy did not want to be in her small town of Misty, Newfoundland, was the local "character" • On my way to work this morning, I saw a bus run over a dog, and the dog's owner howled so loudly that I thought she had been hit by the bus as well, but that wasn't the case • Crystal Manning shaped a glowing green image in her computer cube • I knew it had once been the custom in our family to mark its dead with living wood rather than cut stone, so when my father said we were going to see my grandfather's grave, I found my mouth watering involuntarily at the thought of biting into a sun-warmed apple, fresh from the tree • We had to feed all those animals on the ark and a lot of them weren't herbivores so that meant we had to bring on a secondary group of animals for the primary group to eat • Do the birds all decide at once to fly, is that how it works? • My parents came from Slothin • People say the worst fate you can possibly imagine is to outlive your children, but they're wrong • The night was calm and surprisingly well lit • You might know me as Rhonda Holmes, the author of an influential book on the slippery nature of reality, but you need to know that I don't agree with those that have taken up my theories and distorted them to the point where I have to say publicly that I am *not* a Holmsian • Never make promises, even ones you can keep • Monkeys and crocodiles both taste good • Every story is a survival story • I became a doctor by cheating the system • I've considered the question very seriously for about 20 years and still have not found any good reason to eat artichokes • Laughter didn't cure me, so I have to assume it's not particularly good medicine • Turns out the little guy who lives next door is a Nobel laureate from, like, 40 years ago, who turned his back on physics when it got too weird and then he became a recluse and a pariah • My cat attacked with a ferocity that rivaled a hurricane's fury • The ants formed a chain across the gap between the house and the wasp's nest and I felt sorry for the wasps, but only for a few seconds • When the baby came I stuck it out for a good week, but then it was too much and I split • When Jewel was six years old she asked her mother why the sky was white • Look, it's not my fault you have a skeleton buried inside you • The house leaned to one side, as though it was trying to avoid a puddle • I was new in town, and I didn't have a dog, which made me as conspicuous as a clean shaven man at a beard competition • The man adrift in the street walked in short steps and deflected passing cars with a thin, but apparently invincible, white cane • The snow, alarmingly, was a dark shade of brown, almost purple • The lizard climbed up my wall and onto my roof • I was a Canadian, operating a Mexican restaurant, and that bothered some people • The only thing I want to know about you, about anyone, is what you taste like • My too-large house sits on a property so expansive that the village of my birth would fit comfortably within its confines • Colette spent her days, through no choice of her own, taking care of others • No one saw me • My mouth waters at the smell of pen ink • Every street in our town is a hill • I forgot how to ride a bicycle, which scared me so bad my hands shook for an hour after I fell off of one • The room felt like it was inhabited by some dark beast with intentions counter to my survival • It does a leader no good at all if he gains a reputation for kindness • It wasn't aliens that hijacked the moon, but dead people, hordes of them • Yeah, I worked for the mob for a few years, but I *swear* I didn't *know* Ratface Skalorky was a mobster, not then • I can tell he's a jumper by the way he keeps looking nervously into the dark corners of my office, suspicious like • Brutal as he was, I had a lot of sympathy for the dictator • My hair started falling out during my son's trial • Death has its attractions, that's all I'll say • Varmints got to be killed and that's the truth and everyone knows it • Nothing enrages me as much the public's need to make heroes out of murderers • My brother Jerry grew up with his dog • There was no wind, none at all, just before the rains came • "What will you do when the winds die?" • Shiatsu five-point detection • I was accused of murdering a building • I was a suspect in the murder of Frank Houser • Before she arrived, I cleaned the house until it was a gleaming specimen of super polished excuses for my behavior the previous week • I generally make myself look bad • The boy could not have been more than ten years old • The deceivers were everywhere • Did you notice how I start out with a big fat D? • Hugh's house was a modest thing, made for someone much more poor than he was • Nedra had hopes for her blind date that were less than realistic • She made me turn my eyes away from her eyes, the way they were too wide by half, not to mention how they contrasted with the horns growing out of her skull, just behind her greenish ears • First week you're sick you get a lot of sympathy and visitors, but that doesn't last • Dad said I didn't cry when I was born so I shouldn't cry now, but that sounded like bullshit so I told him I didn't believe him and he slapped me hard • Dron's brain had been strung across the dimension like so much unravelled string • I didn't *have* to break into the house, but it felt right • The aliens didn't fool anyone except the entire human race • Assa grew up in an enchanted land, believing she would become a teacher and perhaps marry and have children of her own • The worms were bad enough, carpets of the squirmy things everywhere in May and June, but when they became moths we were constantly inundated with them, flying around our heads like we were light sources and they were intent on killing themselves on our bright burning faces • Two months ago, when he first noticed the rip in his favorite shirt, it upset him so much that he sulked for an entire day • The clouds came down from the hills and filled the gorge • My request for restitution did not conform to the stringent requirements of the department, which meant I would have to redo it and go back and stand in line again and wait 12 days • I never accept invitations to people's houses because they will expect reciprocation and my house is not fit to be seen by anyone • Don't look for adulation from your own family, no matter how accomplished you become • I had a third eye, but it was blind • Chantilly was a wild child and her aunt was determined to tame her • My grandfather admired the general, but my father knew the general to be a wicked man, and so they did not talk about him, even though he was the leader of our country and about to take me for his army • The director of the play is the puppet master • Over at the language lab Earl had discovered a way to graft an incomplete sentence onto an interrupted thought, thereby creating not only a fully formed cognitive event, but also demonstrating the essentials of language and thought, at least for the inhabitants of that realm the press had dubbed "The Looking Glass Land" • Like the early voyagers, the ones who didn't know what was happening to them, I spend most of my day, up to twenty hours or more, asleep • My husband, Deek, never understood my passion for poker • If a person falls from a high enough distance onto a hard surface they don't break, they splash • Rich ate slowly • Whenever I'm feeling down I go to a stranger's funeral and listen to the eulogies and imagine they are saying all those nice words about me • It was an epic traffic jam, so large and long that I seriously considered getting out of my car and abandoning it, since it was an old junker anyway • I spent most of my post war years as a mute • Kids with tough lives don't always let on what they're going through • Some folks are born thieves, it's how nature made them, and they shouldn't have to apologize for it • The clown died under suspicious, but no less funny, circumstances • Be sad if you need to, but know that sadness wrecks everything • It used to be, when a spouse died, the surviving partner politely retreated from society and nursed his or her grief for as long as it took • I stepped in some blood, a lot of it, and that's when I knew I was in trouble • The criss-cross cobweb of lines on my palm intrigued the fortune teller, or so I thought, until my wife, sitting beside me, abruptly stood and said she wasn't feeling well and had to retreat from the tent to our cabin • Bricks weigh a lot more than you'd think • Joelle told me it took a special kind of person to want to stay on Earth after almost everyone else had left it • He was one of those weirdoes that still took pictures with a film camera and what was worse was that he was insufferably superior about it • My uncle, I am not kidding, cooked and ate skunk, and thought nothing of it • Reality is not what you think it is • The plague years were very good to me, but I keep that fact to myself • When I entered the square I was 11 years old and when I walked out of the square I was near 70 • I explained to the fallen angel that I had certainly seen better days • My father was a proud veteran of World War II, but during Vietnam, he helped me escape to Canada and told me, years later, that he never regretted it for an instant • I had to put a contract on my neighbor's dog • The second time I saw Rebecca reminded me of the first time, 34 years earlier, when she was my friend, before she became my enemy, which is something much more complicated and interesting • My friend Jake was in the mood for some vandalism and asked me if I wanted to come with him • Driving south to Arcata, on California's Highway 101, Evelyn saw the city of golden light floating above the road, high in the sky • Every day the sun comes up and it makes Karl wonder if it ever gets bored • The last cockroach on Earth sat alone in a room • Carrots you raid from a neighbor's garden taste way better than anything you can get in a store, any store • Later I heard people call it the Wild West, but for those of us who lived there, it was just a hot dusty time, day after endless day • I only needed some salt and some bread and I would be set • The predominant life form on the planet was a species of stationary fibrous vegetation that provided the entire surface with oxygen • Don't try to regulate luck • Why make diamonds when you can steal them? • He had a way with horses—gentle, firm, effortlessly in control—that made me think he would be right for what I had in mind • Your parents have limited resources, no matter how rich they are and no matter how needy you are • You should never tell a story in the second person • I had the assassin in my sights, as he had me in his • Utopia harms everyone • I had a well-paying job, much to my dismay • The anarchists wanted me to be one of them • I sometimes wonder if the sun *wants* to shine so bright or if it's just a dreary job it has to do • I was so poor, nothing in the dollar store was within my means • My favorite Peanuts character was Schroeder, but Lucy had her points • Once there was a code breaker who worked for a government besieged by a foreign power intent on dominating her country • In our little town burglary was just a way to fight off the boredom until we could get high again • My life, as the phrase would have it, is an open book • Maybe you don't believe a story can be told in 12 words • Lucy liked dragon meat best of all and her dad was the best dragon hunter in the world • The dog was old and smelly and no one wanted to take care of it and we were going on vacation and didn't want to take her, so you can guess what happened next • When I'm on a train, it takes very little mental gymnastics to imagine the world crawling under the wheels of my car, trailing land behind me • My most accomplished photo, the one that made me famous, the one that made my reputation as a documentary photographer, was staged • Once I moved into the house, I got to know the ghosts that lived there, and they were an okay bunch except for the one who had it in for me in a way I would not understand for some time • The doctor's office room smelled of cigarette smoke • Money didn't change me, but it changed everyone else around me, and not for the better • Darryl's apartment reflected a life of shabby dreams and even shabbier accomplishments • Continue your quest for immortality after you've had a few life experiences that you didn't get from a book • There's no such thing as plenty of money • Me and my buddy Ray did the rock paper scissors thing to see who was going to have to kill our buddy Gabe • The counting begins after Caryn's father dies • All of life, every bit of it • The windows were getting weary of guiding light into the tea room • Noise doesn't bother me too much, but bright lights, they can make me want to kill people • My friends don't get me • There are no true stories, at least, not any that matter • When my son turned 21, I presented him with a bill for his upkeep and education but I wasn't a tyrant about it and told him I would accept monthly payments • The hotel lobby was lousy with academics, conspiracy theorists, journalists, exobiologists, astronauts, flat earthers, and porters • We sent our daughter out into the world, equipped with stamina, smarts, and even some cash, but she came tumbling back less than a year later, her heart broken and begging us to take her back, which we did, much to everyone's regret • I told him to stop calling me and just text me, like a normal person, like the pioneers used to do • Karen turned her face to the rising sun and waited for another day to assault her • *You're just half a person without your twin* • Being a contemplative couple, we thoroughly discussed the matter of children and decided my husband was going to carry our baby to term • The plane crashed and I drew in a sharp breath • Monsters come in twos • We were so thirsty that we set up nets on poles to catch some of the morning mist • Linda never did like the idea of the universe winding down to a flat field more or less infinite in all directions, with only the flash of gamma ray bursts punctuating the eons of nothing as all the black holes evaporated • It's best to not be wedded to marital bliss • When Lindy was 12 years old, an hour after her father died, her mother asked her to fetch the butcher and have him come dress her father's body • A quick scan of my sensors revealed that someone had planted a bomb in my skull while I was asleep and had set it to go off in half an hour, when I was supposed to be in a meeting with the secretary of state • The security line was too slow, so I started heckling the guards • Garon's only hint that something was not right with the world was a persistent and annoying twitch in his lower back • My parents loved me mostly out of obligation and the sense that society demanded it, but their hearts were never in it • My genre was dream creation • I took the last piece of pie, and since it was my *third* piece, everyone looked at me with contempt as I ate it • No one expected the sky, soft blue blanket, to fall and smother everything, but the worst part was the stars, scratchy burrs that stuck to everything • Three things you should know about blimps before you, like I foolishly did, buy one: first, they don't do so good in the wind; second, they don't do so good in the wind; and third, they don't do so good in the wind • The way I see it, God may not be dead, but he sure as hell could be napping • The rats took up residence in my attic, turning my home into something resembling a house of horrors • We thought we were having a love fest, but not everyone agreed with us • My years as a lawyer taught me lessons no one should have to learn • We took a wrong turn, somewhere, neither of us exactly sure where, and now, as darkness crept in around the car, we had to find a way to safety • At the grocery store Marsha saw a man in the produce section accompanied by his own body • Light taps on my door pull me from my dreams, and I hear my name in loud whispers: "Thora, are you awake?" • Carlos was coming off a marathon sewing session that had lasted an epic 14 straight hours when the significance of the garment he was working on overcame him and he broke down sobbing • Frank climbed the ladder to the roof but did not step off the last rung while he waited for his rapid heartbeat to subside • My daddy, he got guns to perteck us an he use dem on peoples whens he gots to • The lighthouse at Point Samuels was still visibly illuminating the sky in the dim light just before dawn • It was the kind of town that I didn't want to be in and that didn't want me • My sculptural self-portrait, being a nude, inevitably raised questions about my anatomy that the gallery owner was too polite to ask • The case of explosives rattled around in my trunk as I took curves with maybe a little too much speed • The pattern was way too busy for a dining table • Fred Martin, retired forester and world champion loafer, never wanted to raise a kid • The fragrance of lavender was so sweet Flint had to brace himself against the possibility of falling from dizziness as it rose up to his nostrils and slithered into his head like a ghostly snake • My heart was my business until I got a summons • I kept the key in a small box tucked in the back of my junk drawer, and never once, in 30 years, thought of using it to open the storage unit it was made for • Mengele was my hero for a long time, until I realized he was far too timid • I told you stories from the time you were born • I was late, true, but I explained to Hannah that it wasn't my fault, even though, objectively speaking, it absolutely *was* my fault all the way • All four passengers on the stage had their guns out • Jennifer dreamed she was playing online Scrabble with an anonymous player whose profile said he or she was in Ethiopia • Once the mine came to Bisbee, there was no place for an honest thief like myself, so I moved on to Nevada where a guy could make a fast buck without hurting anyone • Nothing sexier than a man who knows how to cook and isn't afraid to show it • The spread of human beings throughout the known universe began in a time that most alive could not remember • One day at the library, Japenga Carn noticed something odd • Why am I telling you any of this? • The quality of bread, many people don't realize, is very dependent on the weather when it was baked • It took me a few minutes after I woke up to remember that I was on a spaceship, and that if it had roused me from hibernation there was an emergency that would require my attention • Evil demands maintenance • The last thing you want to see on your wedding day is an old boyfriend • My question is what do you wanna go to Mars for? • The door was broken in three places • Don't underestimate the power of tribal love, even in a gang • Immortality thrives when the worms have a lot to eat • A lot of folks, along about the time they turn 60 or so, they find more comfort in food than in people • The name of the game was shame • I got nothing against people, so long as they are dead • They found him, days later, floating face down in an eddy that circled endlessly, turning his body into a stately second hand, counting off time he could no longer lay claim to • I was ordered to behead the king • First thing that happened is the hourglass fell • Flo liked nothing better than digging through sand and rocks, looking for archaeological treasure • Iceland is rockier than a foundering celebrity marriage • Her encounter with the lost child didn't help the police one bit • Salvador Dali was my neighbor • They said I was going to be executed no matter what, but if I confessed fully, they would make sure it was painless rather than excruciating • The lawyer was doing a good job making me look like an upstanding citizen, a task I wouldn't wish on my worst enemy • The water invaded my lungs like some creature I had thought was fossilized but which came alive at the worst possible moment for me • My clock ate time • I never liked seeing pictures of myself from when I was a kid • Arms dealers have little sentimentality, even concerning very young children • No one should have to put up with a crying baby unless that crying baby is theirs and this one was definitely not • People talk about great men, but not so much about great women • We ended the exercise only because Marlene, the youngest of us, decided she couldn't continue the cruelty through the night • I'm not the type of person to tell you things you already know • The item in the lost and found section of the classifieds caught Joan's attention •

"Where did the eyes come from?" Gary asked Dr Hanes • Doug Anders wrote his last song 30 years ago • Never tell your parents anything about your real life unless you want them to totally freak • Bears smell like nothing you've ever experienced unless you've been married to some fat old guy who doesn't bathe and sleeps all day • I saw the plane drop out of the sky • I like the thought of living with monks that don't speak for weeks on end • The dress, once a vibrant red, had faded to a dull pink which reminded Emily of an old nightmare in which bubble gum had covered the world • It wasn't a guy in black holding a scythe, no, it was, rather, a black horse with wide eyes and a tattooed tongue coming at me with bright lightning bolts carved into its hooves, pounding and thundering the ground • When I'm in the forest I wish the trees would speak up more • Thinking is a very important thing that all people do • When my mother died, neighbors who I more or less couldn't stand, brought us food • I like going back to the factory where I was made, just for nostalgia's sake • You should share your grief, just like you should share your joy • That was about the time I started wearing fluorescent orange eye shadow • The baby knew more than it was letting on • I had a psychic and a geologist in my house one week, an unholy alliance, to say the least • Everyone thinks they're smart, *everyone* • George Campbell, better known to the world as The Amazing Beli, was halfway through his second performance of the evening • Garth told the cops what he saw, but neither of them wanted to listen to a six-year-old kid, even if he was a prodigy • Daureen knew what it took to get ahead, she just didn't have the stomach to do any of it • Countries sin all the time • The thing about hostages, in my experience, is that after a few days they get to be a pain and you have to take measures to keep them in line • Everything, or almost everything, happens for a reason, probably • The milk had turned and the windows were gray • I've always thought the word *frightening* should be spelled without the *e*, so it rhymes with *lightning* • Hood River at night feels like an afterthought of the world • I used to watch our pigs and envy them their simple lives • My mom sometimes called people she didn't like *feather muckers*, but I knew what she really meant to say • The rifle arrived in the mail, just as the founders and the constitution intended • I made bullets by hand and sold them one at a time, priced for the collector's market, signed and numbered • Adrian kept a vivid memory of his outer layer peeled back and the circuitry and infrastructure underneath revealed to his still developing eye in what he took to be a lab: harsh lights, antiseptic stainless steel benches, tools and wires and bolts strewn about • The aliens were beautiful in all ways to children • We made our future child's

DNA into an open source wiki • Don't talk to me about the morally right thing to do, not when I'm holding a gun on the guy that shot my daughter • She wasn't the first woman to come out west disguised as a man, but she had a fair shot at being the purdiest • No one *needs* ice cream, but we still gotta have it • No one cares about me because I was the *second* kid born on Mars, right after my twin brother Ares became the first and most famous of all Martians • I feel like I could have a very full life as a pet • The bus stop had been vandalized overnight • I called them my 52 best friends, but, like real life friends, a deck of cards can betray your loyalty and devotion and make your life miserable • We were both legally blind but it was still love at first sight • Four of us kids stood in front of Old Man Gustafson's house, daring each other to be the first to go up to the door for trick or treats • Air Force One, practically all that was left of the US government, was running out of fuel with no place to land on a North American continent rotted by a fast-moving, unstoppable super fungus • The egg rested on the sand near the spit of rock that jutted into the ocean like a dart • We always liked going to see the windmills • Charlaine was not used to talking to a group, and it showed: her face was pale, and her eyes, wide and almost blank, registered fear • No religion I've encountered does justice to the human impulse for transcendence and spiritual experience •

The restaurant was the sort of place that shouldn't be serving food to anyone • I was surprised to learn that no one remembered anything of their time in the womb • I always have sausages in the fridge because I want sausages to be part of my last meal • The power of money transcends the power of love, or so my grandmother told me just a few days before she died • I always considered snow one of the crowning achievements of creation • My neighbor tells me to watch out for terrorists and keeps urging me to buy a gun, any gun, just to get my feet wet • You had a gig in this podunk town in Idaho that you never heard of but that your manager said would be good exposure • Dylan Everfort became a lawyer the same day he committed his first felony • Janet comes out of sleep confused and disoriented, with one thought: *Something is wrong* • Summer doesn't just sit quietly, it kind of leaps into your head and finds ways to make you as uncomfortable as it can because that's what summer likes to do • The invaders were mostly bad people, I know, but I still couldn't help falling in love with one of them • His last words to me were so banal that later, when I wanted to write them down, I couldn't remember them • The one thing I can't abide in my fellow human beings is rancid breath • The worst part, by far, is that I'm the only one of my kind • The party was just getting started when the earthquake made its sudden and over-the-top entrance • The dictator's family was not going to save him • The department store was big enough that it had its own weather • The recipe had its deficiencies • It's no one's fault but God's that I hate my family but I love my dog • We began with spoons, scooping dirt out one spoonful at a time • The officer was clearly bored by the way my house had been invaded and destroyed • The guy on the bus who just *had* to sit next to me smelled of rotten fish and weeks-old body odor and it was all I could do to keep from throwing up • For one disconcerting moment I thought the ceiling was bleeding • Even up to the day she died, Oscar made sure he never dressed better than his wife • I had work I cared about and then they fired me for caring too much • The body was smelly • Ken supposed most revolutions began with a group of people getting together to air their gripes • I prayed that I would never have to be brave • Fasting was never my friend • Potatoes are the ultimate • My evil twin loved money • My name is Michael Karass and you have to know two things about me: first I'm a kid in middle school and second I can fly like a bird • The aliens lived off by themselves which suited everyone, including the aliens • The city loved me, but only for a short time • I had a safe house on the underground railroad that smuggled alien babies out of the secret government nursery and into the submarine that took them down to the ocean depths where they could grow up strong and angry • Last night I had acute pain from my inguinal hernia which I tried to push back in, but which would not go back no matter how much I labored at it • When your parents don't want you, you will always feel like a foreigner no matter where you are • I had serious thoughts of stepping in front of the guy with the gun, but in the end, the store clerk was going down and I wasn't going to be added to the list of victims • The guests, when they arrived, brought snow and encrusted ice with them • The party lasted the better part of three days and four nights • The storm was not the sort of thing we much noticed in our part of Alberta, but it did signal the arrival of a new order, one destined to make life miserable for everyone far and wide • The room was cold • The meal had a lot of bug ingredients • Why anyone would drink coffee is still a profound mystery to me • The glories of spring were muddied by the arrival of the yellow jackets • Lora had been dead ten years, but I still talked to her whenever I went out into the woods • I always liked dead end streets, which is why I put my mortuary on one, a joke, of sorts, that not everyone appreciated, death being one of those things that drains the sense of humor out of just about everyone • Farrah had seen enough suicides in her life that this one—a boy no more than 16—shouldn't have bothered her, but it did • Five minutes before closing, Edwin made the rounds of the library, waking the drunks that had taken shelter from the cold outside, gently reminding people in the stacks that it would soon be time to leave, and generally causing a commotion in his wake as people scurried to gather up papers and pens, close notebooks, stuff all into briefcases or knapsacks, and struggle into overcoats and gloves, all of which gave him a pang of guilt as he snapped off the circuit breakers one by one, replacing the stark white fluorescent brightness with a pleasantly dim gray • The door was made of stone • Text me, Ishmael • On some evenings, melancholy ones, the night, as it approaches, feels like some entity eating light and trailing darkness behind it • Say what you want • I had a need for revenge so strong that I asked my brother to keep me confined for a week, a request he refused, giving some kind of balderdash about freedom as his reason, which only infuriated me even more • Mules are beautiful creatures • Probably the best time to run away from home is around two in the morning, after everyone else in the house is asleep, and a goodly number of hours before the sun comes up • My peculiar ability was seeing the phantom limbs of amputees • Love never wins • She expected to die even before she washed up on the Florida coast, but that did not happen • New York has everything, or, at least, it used to, before things changed • I had a clutch of gold coins and I didn't want any of it to lose its value by becoming anything less than rare, so you can see why I *had* to put a hit on that over-producer Rumpelstiltskin • Never look at a city from the air because it's all just ugly rooftops • My neighbors were the kind of people that liked anyone who owned a dog • Guitar strings always break at the worst time possible • People get all worked up about cheating, like it's something bad • The woods covered their country and it was a simple thing to deploy a hundred or so soldiers with torches to set the entire nation aflame • There are two kinds of people in the world: those that divide folks into categories, and those that don't • My father was a hunter and when I turned vegetarian I thought I would make him angry but instead I broke his heart • The door looked like it had been scratched by a big cat, maybe a mountain lion • A suicidal tendency in old age may sometimes be attributed to depression, but not always • Ha ha ha ha ha ha ha ha ha • The year I fasted I also didn't wear any clothes and spent no time in-doors, just to see if the planet wanted me to stay alive • The visitors asked us, in a most casual and informal manner, if they could eat our cat • The landscape outside the car window seemed overrun by ghostly white shapes, shadows from Richard's mind, floating over the desert night • I decided I would stay on the job until I fell over and became a bit of debris like a dried out husk of an insect, a cockroach maybe, which would disgust anyone who found me • Above Clearwater Lake there's a bench for me to sit on and watch what's left of Mount St Helens • The book was overdue by 42 years and three months • Renaldo made a mean omelet • The drum was made of deerskin, but its sound betrayed no hint of a prey's wildly beating heart • The lizards • "You'll see it when you believe it," was what my mother told me whenever I doubted myself • I made a mental list of all the items in my room that could do double duty as weapons • The master sat behind his desk, as nervous as Norma, though this was not immediately apparent to her • One mountain is as good as another, I suppose, since they all try to leave the world, clad in wedding dress white, like they want to elope with the sky • They hung a child abuse label on me like there was something wrong with what I did • Greeta talks to her god while I wait patiently for her to finish • Aaron always kept his revolver close by, even when he was at work, even when he was in the restroom, and even when he was sleeping • Home was a long way off, and there were snipers lining the streets, and he was tired of them and decided he was going to risk walking in their line of fire, just this once • The crucifix meant nothing to me, which was a point of friction between me and my devout wife • You take a photocopy of a photocopy of a photocopy and keep doing that for a hundred times or so and then you look at what you have and you don't know what you have • Though I had seen Gerard Raynor the night before, I had officially left his project several months earlier, so the phone call from the detective came as a mild surprise • You come to my office a smoker or way overweight, I'm going to tell you straight up I don't spend a lot of time wasting my expensive medical education on people that want to die • My cousin called me up, like we were best buds, only I didn't remember him and he got insulted and said I was a disgrace to the family • My food cart was the best on the block and I didn't understand why I wasn't getting any customers • Draper Lichess, he of the long tangled locks and grimy overcoat, was one of our regulars • I thought of my predilection for crying as a weapon, but no one else did • When the time came, I was surprised that I actually wanted my last meal to be something special • My dad always said I should laugh in the face of danger because then, if things went bad, I'd be laughing as I passed Satan on my way to hell, and Satan hates laughter, just *hates* it with a passion • Hector told me to call them locomotives, not trains, and I went along with his suggestion just to keep the peace • I slapped my kid's hand a lot until I found out some people think that's abuse • Grief moved in and outstayed its welcome by at least six months, maybe more • I have always felt homeless • Lori was lonely again • Given her looks, and her exceptional intelligence, no one who knew Dominique ever expected her to have trouble in life • Sometimes a person has to choose between keeping a loved object and selling it for the money to buy food • The porch was so cold I could see my breath • The laws of space were changed in the early years of the 23rd century, which meant that the descendants of Neil Armstrong now owned the moon • She had a mean left jab and an even meaner knee to the crotch, all of which I can report from personal experience • No shoe store in town had shoes big enough for my feet, a fact that elicited from shoe store employees various degrees of amusement, respect, disgust, and horror • The path tested Calista's resolve to the breaking point • When my sister Ariel was seven, she got a cancer that no one on Mars could cure, so our parents took her to Earth—*totally* against her will—and made her be three times heavier than normal while the doctors worked on keeping her alive and, she told me later, she cried non-stop practically the whole time • Communist Yugoslavia in the 1950s never saw a comrade more loyal or hard working than Simo Nemchek • Carol got the call in the early evening, just as she was about to sit down to dinner with Roth • Writing novels is no respectable occupation for anyone, much less someone in their 80s • You don't want to give me money, that's fine, it's a free country, mostly, and you can just walk on by without delivering any kind of lecture or insult, thank you very much, because first of all I don't need it, and second of all, I've heard them all before, every one of them and you aren't going to come up with anything different no matter how smart and *superior* you think you are • Families sometimes spawn monsters • My dog always knew when bad weather was coming • I envied the old lady and her shoe—at least she had a roof over her head • Time dilation meant it had been something like five centuries since I had visited my home planet • I think I traced my need to hide back to my father • I did my thesis on a painting by an obscure artist from Canada who painted nothing but butterflies, thousands of them, all wrong in at least one detail • The trees were everywhere, like a plague, choking out everything else • Starships are grungy places • The ship was taking on water at an alarming rate and the captain ordered all hands to bailing while he charted a course to Lisbon, hoping it was still a safe place to effect repairs • In winter, on the Southern Oregon Coast, the Pacific Ocean challenges its own name by turning into a restless leviathan concocted of white-capped waves, wind- and mist-saturated air, and crashing water churning up the beach sand like a giant creature digging its claws into the Earth to reset the moorings of the planet • We found a working watch at the bottom of the well • I helped the hangman adjust the noose around my neck for a nice snug fit and told him it was a good day to die and thanked him for his service • The pool water was murky with bits of trash floating on the surface, making it look like a scene from a minor version of hell • The birds • Babies get way more respect than they deserve • No one liked the doctor • I had a T-shirt with Alice's face on it over the words "EAT ME" but no one got it and my teacher made me go home to change into something different but I thought fuck it and walked out of school and went and ate some ice cream instead • "Here, try this one," said Darcel, and handed Linette a paper maché mask from the trunk • We solidified the sun's rays and planted the resulting golden spikes in a circle around the temple • The coup was going well until the president, who should have been secured in his cell, escaped and killed one of the guards, which enraged the leader of the coup, who then recaptured the president and subjected him to the most vile of tortures, broadcast to the nation as a stern warning • Paulette and I were having lunch at Max's, the best restaurant around—according to the owner • The production was without a chorus member that night and I was pressed into duty, walking the boards, even though I had never been on stage and had no desire to do so • You probably don't know much about dust, but you should • I ran the shell game on my corner for several months as I gathered data for my thesis • Nothing will keep you from your rightful wealth more than sympathy for the poor • No one wants to hear about your operation • She gave her nationality a bad name by adhering to all the cliches that should never have defined her or her people • I found her on the sidewalk near my house, thinner than clear soup, looking more fragile than a soap bubble • Max tried to live in Phoenix one summer without access to air conditioning • All the kings and all the queens of the world held a summit • When the college which had rejected my application so many years ago called and asked me to accept an honorary degree and give a speech I told them to fuck off • You got big doers and you got little doers and all in all I prefer the little doers because they don't mess up the world • At their core, all religions are simple because they all say the same thing: don't be a jerk • Dreams are boring but no one wants to admit it • It's not prejudice if you know the person and hate them for being that person rather than for being part of an ethnic group and it's not love if you love a person because they are part of an ethnic group you admire • Gavin's idea of beginning a conversation was to announce his topic as though he was delivering a proclamation • Remi was tired • I checked the numbers so many times I knew them by heart, but still I didn't claim the lottery win for many weeks, thinking it might be best to remain a simple laborer rather than a multi millionaire • I visited my neighbor's native country once, but that was enough to turn me into a bigot, a fact for which I can conjure no apologies and no shame • Everyone talks about the universe like they know the first thing about it • First of all, no matter what you think, lawyers don't care about the truth, trained, as they are, in the practice of advocacy at any price • The tigers • I saw things on the trail that would make your eyes melt • Oddballs, we were, raised on a meager diet of hope and withheld affection • The pen held blood, not ink • The cockroach with the stylized lightning painted on its back was slightly ahead, but another cockroach, with a race car stenciled on its back, was moving up fast and was about to overtake the first cockroach when Ted told me he wanted to change his bet • Owen Deerfield, age 26, had one love in his life: Space Invaders • First, please understand that we did not ask for the foundling • The wildfires sent so much smoke into the air that the sun was an orange hanging in the sky • Time was the best, then it was the worst • My daughter was trapped in the mirror • Johanna learned how to embezzle money from the accountant who stole from her mother • You take a human being, a physical entity made of flesh, blood, bone, drive, and heart, then squeeze out their essence by some quantum physical mumbo jumbo, slip that essence onto the data stream, and shoot the stream into space, and, well, you no longer have a human being, at least not to Grant Keyson's way of thinking • The poet in the corner looked like she was going to disappear into the furniture • You tell two people your secret and one laughs, but the other, the one who says "me too," that one is, without question, a member of your tribe, whether you like it or not • Families don't want you to succeed too much because they fear disintegration • My opinion: babies shouldn't be in prison

The middle: below the surface

The iceberg was a city unto itself. Inhabited by so many tribes, we took to calling it the ice burg. The captain ordered me to enter the ice city and she was not kidding.

I dutifully donned my winter clothing and put spikes on my boots, the better to scramble over the ice. As I boarded the small boat that would take me from my beloved ship *The Hidden* to the ice, the captain leaned over and told me all would depend on what

I found. Such pressure was difficult to take in. "I will do my best," I said.

"Your best is not enough here," she said. "You must do more than your best. Understand?"

I did not, but told her I did.

When I arrived, I was greeted by a pack of dogs. They lived on the ice. At first I was terrified, but then I saw they were not there to attack, but rather to escort.

We were dogs, it was true, but not bloodthirsty. Life on a slab of ice kills that instinct. The visitor would have been tasty under other circumstances. Instead we escorted her to the first chamber, where we all stood on the ice, sheltered by ice walls and a roof of ice. None of the dogs spoke, at least not then. If we did, we were sure we would have scared the visitor half to death.

Instead we arranged ourselves in a circle around her and took our repose, panting slightly, but with an air of benevolence that we had practiced and perfected during our many years on the ice.

The visitor introduced herself.

"I am Rada," she said.

We nodded. No words from us, though.

"I am here to ask for help."

We knew that, but we were not going to be her helpers. One of us barked as a way of showing support. She took it as danger and jumped back. Her spikes caught in the ice and she fell over.

Just about that time, the Ice Queen arrived.

I had not expected a visitor from the ship anchored within sight of my floating city to come to us so soon. However, I knew it was going to happen, and I had prepared. The dogs were on their best behavior. I made sure a slip was prepared for the visitor's boat. And I kept the rabble tucked deep inside the ice.

"Hello," I said to the visitor.

She bowed. Someone must have told her I required such gestures.

"No need for that," I said. "Just address me as Queen."

"Queen," said the visitor, "I humbly ask for your aid."

"And what aid do you require?" I knew exactly what she wanted, but I also wanted her to ask me first.

"Our ship is failing. There is no wind. The hull is breeched. We are sinking. We have only a few days. May we board the ice?"

The ice, the ice. They all hate the ice. Until they need it.

"Life here is—different."

"I understand."

"I don't think you do," she said. "You and your crew may live here, but you need to know that the rabble that lies at the heart of the ice, they are unruly. They will try to do you harm."

The visitor looked uneasy, as though she just realized her world was broken.

"The ice is vast. You see only a tiny fraction. So much of it under the surface. Unknown and unknowable. It is a vast uncharted wilderness. The ice has been here for centuries and there are tunnels and chambers that go for miles."

The visitor looks up at me. She knows I speak the truth but she does not want to hear it. Any of it.

"We have heard stories," she says. "So many stories."

"All of them are true."

The visitor does not know what to say. But then she opens her mouth and begins to sing. The dogs all perk up. Their ears twitch and their throats tremble and before long they are all howling along with her.

My own heart, frozen since I was born on the ice, began to melt.

Us dogs saw the queen relent. She was not going to refuse the request for aid. It didn't matter. The ice had room for so many. We sang in unison, all our voices merging into one. The ice reverberated around us. The ice rang with our singing. So much ice. Everything tucked away for the future. So much exploration. The queen's eyes welled up with tears. The songs we sang. The notes we reached.

Survival depended on my singing. I sang better than I had ever sung before. The dogs with me. And, finally, the queen. Her voice joining ours. The brightness of her face. The glow in her eyes. The love that came forth. All from my singing.

And then the rabble, boiling up from below. All of them coming to listen, but many coming, also, for something more sinister.

The queen turned to the mob and raised her hands.

Endings: above the surface

Endings are hard • And they all lived sappily every after • The ea-
gles that year were thinner than usual • I knocked on the door • I
never liked that house anyway • In the Hall of Mosses, the trees
were lit by the low sun and seemed to be dancing with each other
in bright, yellow clothes • Stopping was out of the question • We
were made by different gods • His cold dead heart • "I have nothing

more to say," uttered the monk, and then he died • "Just call me Killer" • He carried my genes • She pretended not to notice • It isn't here • And he always thought gratitude was overrated anyway • All towns resemble each other if you don't choose to look • The river eventually found the Oregon coast • The accumulating snow • This time there weren't as many of them • There was no time for a eulogy • Luv U 2 • She was a good cat • He was a drunk and there is nothing more to say about him • But dreams mean nothing to the Ganymedians • I took up the sword and felt its weight and the soul of the smith who forged it • It wasn't just my imagination • "My choice," she said • But it was all, *all of it,* there in his eyes • The duck bothered me at first, but then: nothing • Which told you more about the egg than you needed to know • Gray, nothing but gray as far as I could see • In that way, it was easy to mistake the light for knowledge • "It's yours" • It was no one's fault but mine • All the cats raised a fuss simultaneously • I could see I had a tough fight ahead of me, but I adjusted my attitude and set myself to the task • None of it was real, but I believed all of it • With each next to the other, they headed south • I sidestepped any impulse to think it through and dove in • The stranger called my name • He waited a long time, savoring the anticipation, before he made his feet move from their spot and picked up the garment and held it, worn and weathered, like an old woman's skin, up to his trembling nostrils • Some considered it in bad taste • I did not testify against my husband, but in the end it was my bruises—numerous and ugly—that betrayed him • The carpet proved to be less than adequate • But just before he did, he raised the weapon high so it discharged its shots into the ceiling, and dust and shards of plaster fell on all three of them, so they looked like ghosts, each blinking bright eyes at one another as though the world had disappeared for a moment and they had to get their bearings before they could move on • I ate every last bite • Too weary of it all • Inside the box was a piece of wrapping paper • The name—remember this—was Norton Humphrey Bellagerits • I pulled the cord and the chainsaw coughed and sputtered, but would not start • I will bring her home • We heard all this through other people's ears • The googly eyes said it all • The grass was green and cool and dry • Considering the source of the rumor, there was no reason to believe it from the get go • We can take care of each other • I have never told anyone else in the world where I hid it • That was how we justified the killing • She never was much good at reading people's faces • I walked away and never turned back • The watch slips out of her hand and falls to the river below • But only Nadia saw that something bad was coming • No reason to think otherwise • Destruction was not my best look • The horses were ready and so were we • I kept the change • I scanned his temperature and circulation readings, then invoked my sympathy protocols and told him everything was going to be okay • But it was knowledge only the two of them shared, and they kept it to themselves forever after • No one wishes for that kind of future • Sooner or later my cough was going to kill me and everyone else in the group • The life jackets saved us, exactly as they should, but it still felt like a miracle • I pressed the button • The band picked up the tune, and kept playing the rest of the night • We cried for some time • "You'll have my decision in the morning," she said • We found out where the pain goes when you die • But in my circle, we don't call that murder • We watched the mountain lion go up the hill until she melted into the surrounding woods • We collapsed toward the morning and waited a long time for the sun to come up • I shot him • I was willing to help, this time • But nature, in her way, does keep score • Gratitude came later • And in their odd eyes, a sense of fear mixed with awe • *Please let him in* • Maybe it is trying to warn me • The hawk rose on a thermal and was soon out of sight • My memories of those days will never fade • He had the director's full support at all times during the operation • The cage, at least, was sturdy • He paused on the front steps, took a big breath, let it out slowly, and tapped a seven note melody with his knuckles on Lynn's door • I could have used a hundred grand • Like my grandfather told me: everyone's got to make a living, even crooks • That's what people want • I passed by the occupied parking space—that had been meant for me—with a wistful sense of what might have been • It only leads to trouble • I ate well that night • The sound, brutal as it was, eventually healed itself • He left a hundred dollar tip • A small tattoo of an apple on her right wrist • Thousands of them • So cold she was fatigued from all her shivering • The stream held a pair of ducks, swimming among the reeds growing up through the water along the shore • The sea was a color I could not name and did not recognize • The screen • I took in a deep breath and held it, waiting for her signal to exhale • I liked it that way • "It will hurt," I said, "but only a bit, and then—nothing" • Nothing to save him now • I could not look at her, not the way she was • Well, okay then • A dead bat plastered to the grill of my car • She made me happy • The cries of my new born daughter echoed off the walls • The crying fathers, all of them • He was used to waiting • I suppose it had to be a yam • But at least there was plenty to eat • And I am grateful that drink never killed me • Infinity is no invitation to despair • Fortunately for me you can't exhume a cremated body • I released my dreams to the world • The universe held surprises, even for Star • Don't come to me with your charity cases • "But friendship," he told me with a distinct sneer in his voice, "can only go so far" • Those few hors d'oeuvres were the only thing I had to eat that entire day • But sleep would not come • The scraping in the wall, so terribly unnerving, went on and on and on • She keeps promising to leave • The sun set that night on a unified Mars • Money gave him the permission he needed • In the end, his efforts on my behalf did not matter • Clouds touch the mountains like snowy fingers • The endless darkness beckoned as I prepared to face my long exile • The coffin was even tinier than I expected • The wine said it all • I planted enough for me and for the animals and for the kids who liked to raid gardens • By the end of the trading day the stock had lost 90 percent of its value • "Something like that," said Therese • The house then owned me and my family • The shadows on his face were the closest he ever came to expressing a poetic thought • Best thing, at the end of a story, is to not be any sillier than you have to be • We had to learn the words • No one expects their blood to sing • The ticket in my hand was all the freedom I needed • No words could possibly explain any of it • But no one applauded the verdict • The sun rose again, bringing the fire of death with it • I chose to listen • Her closet, to everyone's surprise, held several dozen oil paintings she had, apparently, been working on over the last decade and a half •

I would wait until the time was right • The beggar still had hope • "Are you saying you would have preferred a reliable narrator, and if so, should I believe you?" • He decided not to help any of them • The asteroid kept its promise • No sooner than necessary • My business if I use and my business if I die • Eat well, keep your head above water, know your enemies, and—Peace • The sheriff stared down the track, avoiding talk of what they were both thinking • And only Greta to thank • At least she knows she has a friend • He really hated selfies • By then it was much too late • "Care for some biscuits with jam?" she asked in a perfectly sinister voice • I hardly ever miss him • The hope was that the sky would recover its former glory • But I would never recommend you do the same • The meal sealed our pact • None of them ever answered me • You'll see the other side • Keep going • Wishing people well is no use to anyone • Who would think such a thing, ever? • The orders were clear——kill all the survivors—but she chose to ignore them, thus sealing her own gruesome fate • "You'll see" • It was the thumb drive with the portrait of Minnie Mouse on the back • I snapped my fingers and all was dark • And childhood, that lost country, no longer had a reliable map • The servants were kind, something I didn't deserve, then or ever • The diagnosis was ambiguous, at best • I didn't rest until the seventh day • She was the only one who deduced I was a woman in disguise • They slapped me on the cheek, each in turn, then retreated and left me to my misery • We dreamed of maple leaves, felt the texture of them on our tongues, and hummed the music of the cosmos • She was always much too melodramatic • All in all, I have to admit, he was my favorite husband • I was, after all, a midwife to the goddesses • It was his hospital, and he was determined to make it a great one again • There was not enough water in the world to make that plant grow • We drew closer • It was the sound of no hands clapping • We all expected a long dark summer • She raised her glass, but I refused to do the same • The sound consumed everything • He turned his back to me and walked away • Silence kills • Soon Karen and Lee came down from upstairs to see the carnage • It smelled of blood • The awful sound of blood pounding through my head • "That's not my name," she said • No one understands I loved the creep • I've seen the pain • That song again • Fast and shallow in a desperate play for clarity • #letitgo • I knew my father would understand • A single strand of red rope fiber • The turtles lined up all in a row facing me • He told me he was an angel and I was never sure if I should believe him or not • That decisively ended my career in translation • She stepped forward • Like fish gasping for water, drowning in a sea of air • We never saw Sundown Jane again • We began the reconciliation with a case that I knew would break everyone's heart, but I gritted my teeth, pasted on my best genial smile, and looked up from the papers in front of me to see a gaunt man who was staring into infinity and who did not see me and would not see me for the rest of the proceedings • It was my burden then • To rebuild was the only option left • The 6:15 bus came to a halt and let him off • I pushed him into the street and hoped he would be hit by something big, metal, and lethal • I never picked up garbage again • LOADS OVER 14 FEET MUST TURN RIGHT • But like an old fool, he thought love was everything • Thanks for the time spent • Like the great blue heron above her house, she had places to go • But she had nothing more to say to them • Only soft mewling sounds • No such thing as true love • The horses never asked for their fate • The blister on the side of my foot did not hurt nearly as much as I thought it would • I reached into the bag • We drew straws and Lydia was the lucky one this time • The hills were covered in alternating bands of green, yellow, and red • No more tears for the lost years • The creep just sat there, staring at me like a pervert, and I, in return, took a few seconds to prepare my mind and body to beat him down to nothing • We learned later that the woman had suffered a mild heart attack • So many ducks • But then the ghost came back • The hotel collapsed soon after • Anyway, I've always heard you shouldn't end a story with descriptions of weather, no matter how pleasant or appropriate • No need for pride at such a late date in the decline of my country • We had nothing left but the memory of that day • The chair collapsed under his weight • As though everything in her world was exactly as it should be • A kind of beast such as I have never seen before, nor care to see again • He removed his spectacles and faced the bank of muzzles aimed at him with blurry precision and the last thing he heard was the sound of the sergeant's sword slicing air just before he yelled "Fire!" • Nothing left to offer anyone • She wasn't worth listening to • Just regular folk with a grudge to settle • But no description will adequately convey the misery • One bit of truth might be all we get in the end • The light streaming through the stained glass windows gave no comfort • Jan may not have remembered, but I certainly did • She held it up for everyone to see • The laughter was much less joyful than it should have been • The games we played, but never won • I could save some time or I could invest the time, and there was no doubt which I would choose • I did not pray with them • We rushed forward as fast as we could, as though we were going to crash through mirrors • My prayers, while not exactly *answered*, were at least acknowledged • Insomniacs are tiresome • The darkness was all • We all knew enough was never enough, not with him

• Such strange sounds when one is out at night • As good a reason as any to resist the mob • Harv would have a mug of hot chocolate and plate of cookies waiting for me • I did forget about her, mostly • Most of the people here are kind enough • And she thought the whole thing was *funny* • It was the light • I ended the investigation and made sure no one would find out what really happened • And anyway, heaven was never going to be his thing • I hefted the baseball, then turned and threw it in the air so that it arced high over the fence and landed near a kid who grabbed it and held it close to his chest and wouldn't let anyone else see it • We were secure, for now • Not a dragon, okay? • It was a winter to remember • I picked up the check for everyone • So I can say with certainty that even after murder, life will return to normal for everyone, even the victim, in an odd, memory-saturated way • I only hope I never find a friend like him again • He thanked her, which was the last thing she expected from him • Mercury sighed and went to the house to get Charon a blanket • A cup of coffee with cream and sugar, the way the universe intended • He screams • So many footprints everywhere, and none of them was Marcel's • The dirt on the door handle felt gritty as he climbed into the car, put his body against the cool, smooth vinyl, and waited for Kate to get into the driver's seat • A soft chuckle, sprinkled like salt grains, fell upon her and she knew she would never be alone again • He could find no warmth or compassion anywhere within himself • The wind spoke in a language I, miraculously, unexpectedly, understood • The American obsession with royal uteruses continues to this day • His last day on the planet, and he spent it at the library • The glory of a new life • I saw it was a bottle of Cabernet Sauvignon 2014 from Star Lane Happy Canyon of Santa Barbara, which made me very happy • I stepped up to the tee knowing, this time, I would go under par • "It's all right," he said • Once he got going, nothing was going to stop him • My tweet went unnoticed as far as I can tell • That took guts • I switched off the light • Not my fault, any of it • And through the whole affair, I never broke my promise • Not an ending anyone should endure • Sleep followed soon after • The pelicans followed the shore going north • So me and my dad, we used the time left to build a table for the dining room • I didn't feel like a hero, but maybe that didn't matter • I viewed the egg as a premonition, like Magritte • Not such a bad outcome for any of us • After that day, Rand never saw Wade again, though he lived for a very long time • "I don't know," he said, "but I'm glad I tried" • I asked for the same thing • But, of course, that depends on which alias you know me by • The scent of unsmoked tobacco • She holds the rope in her hand as she clambers down the rocky hill to the creek threading its way down to the lake where Tyke and Ina said they would be waiting for her • He was always our most inventive spellcaster • The motorcycles roared to life and moved as one organism onto the freeway where they continued on south toward the border • The dog had an extremely shaggy coat • Carolyn and Dale, clambering down from their perch, alighted on the ruins of their town and rolled up their sleeves and got to work • At night, if I knew where to look, I could see his final resting place crossing the sky in low orbit, lights blinking • I decided no one really understood Ruthanne and no one really needed to • I woke up alone • The exit ramp up ahead could take him off the freeway, away from town, across the prairie, and he would not decide if he would take it until the last possible second • I would have to wait for official confirmation of the body's identity, but I knew • She was never gong to leave that tree • I tried to remember how wonderful life can be, but it was hard • But it was *my* painting and they had no right • Who can possibly know the inner workings of a horse's brain? • And then I saw the missing button, there in the bottom of the trash can • Kissing is all well and good, but it has to *mean* something • I finally recognized where the tear in the sleeve came from • The sky should not have been pink, I knew that much • "Are you my prince?" • It's simple, really: love me, love my parrot • The cup lay shattered on the floor • She wore white • But he was family, so that changed every-thing • He carried her image with him for the rest of his days • Lucky for me the pastor was a friend • The man in the ticket booth seemed to like me after all • I was infuriated when my students asked me if what I just said, which came from the deepest part of my heart and soul, would be on the final exam • I never wanted to see her again • It just felt like the right thing to do • I learned much later that a wolf attacked and killed him • Played pool the rest of the night and on into the morning • I felt sorry for him • We watched the vines climb up the side of the house over the next thirty years and never once felt the need to trim them back • She raised the umbrella over her head against the rain and walked home • I knew what was in the envelope without even looking at it, let alone opening it • The revelation came later • The octopus lay crushed on the road, its tentacles a slippery mess that Megan avoided by walking past it on tiptoe • For once, something I could understand • She never looked better than at her own funeral • The bowl held five rotting oranges • All I could offer the wretched thing was a few seconds of warmth • It was eerie, that feeling • But the house was empty • Not my fault the war was coming • Not even any of mine • That bike carried all my dreams away • "I have no idea," she said • Mermaid chants filled the air • It grew • And I believed that after enough meals, all would be forgiven on both sides • Laura told her all about it • It was a sound to wake the dead, but Kami slept through it • I was not sorry to see them go • No one wanted to hear him anymore • It wasn't much longer after drinking the poison that he died • The footprints in the snow already filling in with new flakes • Open the package now • Oh, right, the humanity, eh? • Never put me on a submarine again • We all knew such an occurrence was never going to happen • The crutches felt comfortable • Always listen to what the stars are telling you • They recorded her death as occurring at seven pm, her least favorite time of day • I filled my pack with enough food to last three days and then stepped onto the trail • All night the talk went on, like a fit of indulgence • I gave off a cool pure light • Striped like the lines of a fence • He cried and cried until the doctors came and took him away • The lights were coming back on and I felt a pang of regret • No one ever did it better • Fate has its own agenda, and always will • Lunch was longer than it needed to be • I decided I would ask the district attorney for his opinion • The eels were tasty that summer • Love is for losers • It always startles me, that noise, as though it is not a natural sound • Buses do matter, don't forget that • They were doomed • I swam thirty laps, nonstop, hoping for an end to the pain, but it never came • I didn't recognize the name on the name tag, even though I knew it was mine • Only I knew it was a lie • It can't be true, it can't be true, it can't be true • The doctors tried, but they had nothing in the end • The jury, I knew, was not on my side anymore • Everything turned out well for me, but that wasn't enough • The elephant's tusk lay uneasy in my basement • How long before he would forget his former master? • "Bang, bang, bang" • He turned so she would not see his tears • Who will ever know? • That's a question no one wants to ask or answer • His alibi, at least, held up • You could say we were just hopeful romantics • My glasses got instantly foggy as I came into the house from the sub-zero cold outside • God does not live in every heart • It was a hard lesson to learn • The expiration date reeked of randomness • She glowed • It had been lying dormant for some time • Never had a better meal in my life • But I couldn't have expected anything better • I swam hard toward the island • That night he taught me everything I needed to know about inflicting unwanted pain • Mountains, in his experience, rarely mourned any loss, much less the loss of a mule • Dreams, in the end, are just dead weight • The bear just sat there, staring at me • No one expected Thor's return • Death always has pride • The bug made a crunching noise under my foot, which made Heath scream, exactly the reaction I was hoping for • She looked no different than she looked all those years ago

• Later, Herman would not remember who had won the game • I fed the oracle my quarter and waited for the card with my fortune to come rolling out of the slot • The paint samples slipped out of her hands and fell to the floor • The fall was slow and leisurely and not at all terrifying until the last few seconds • The museum after dark • But Demitri always knew more than he let on • The fork in the road was still there, right next to the spoon • "Good to be back," said Horace Oates • She was gone • The pure clean taste of blood • Her voice filled the room • My travels took me there, but I did not stay • Practice practice practice • I brought the shovel blade down fast and hard, cleanly severing the snake's head • That was not an option I had considered • The room wouldn't cooperate for at least a week after that • My resolve was tested all the rest of that century • Our term of endearment lasted about seven years • Maggie drove and he dozed • Unlike my suicidal husband, whose name I still curse, I live with my choices • Have to say, I did too • So don't believe this story • Good times, after all, come and go • But I do miss Earth • Soft snow covered her tracks and silenced the world • "What are you going to do now?" • Dying would be the easy part • He had to be alive • I don't believe my forgiveness meant much to him, but I offered it anyway, as a form of comfort for justice denied • It would take me a lot longer to learn the rules • She was right •

So many mirrors and none of them offering any pleasant distortions • Even the window shattering did not rouse me from my retreat to silence • He said goodbye with no conviction behind his words • The wrap party, like most of them, was a depressing affair • No fun being a living legend • I felt them beneath my feet as I kept walking, my nose in the air, alert for the odor of fresh meat • The gears meshed, turned, and ate time • The most awful thing about her murder is that not long after she died I forgot her name • It was his sacrifice, not mine • The interview lasted only two minutes • She died a few years later, perfectly content as her world crumbled to pieces around her • The shoes did not fit, but they would do for now • It sounds ridiculous to say, but it was the best meal I ever had • I took a razor to my scalp • It was a fine looking boat, no doubt of it • He dropped the key on my palm and I closed my fist around it • I chose the door on the left • We began the mural under the thinnest of crescent moons • The river, she decided, had an appetite that she was going to try to satisfy • Bottom feeders, all of them • Faulty premises, all of them • The answer was six • I knew exactly what he meant • The critters still had the love for me • No one was there when I woke up • It tasted better than Dana's pie, that was certain • It felt bad, but only for a few minutes • But there's always a sliver of regret every time you pull a trigger • The words were not there • He filled his lungs and let himself remember some of his day, then pushed it from his mind and concentrated on his driving • Gravel pressed against my soles • Always family • Never been so tired before or since • "I think there's a section on fritters in here," he said to the last patron • I hammer the "For Sale" sign into the front lawn at a spot very close to the sidewalk but away from the driveway • She kissed him • I go out the door, into the cold, and leave my mother behind • Her footsteps • The life of a dog • I pondered that line for many years after • Never expect love from a ghost • I couldn't get to the cup in time and it finished its fall and shattered on the floor, an explosion of chalky white ceramic bits • But everyone knows your first death is your hardest • I doused the flames and stirred the ashes, then turned toward the mountains • So many sighs • I took the steps two at a time • Each one was tasty • My own heartbeat, strong and regular • The owner smiles, showing luminous teeth, and informs the tea drinkers that the secret is all in the presentation • I did decide that when I told the story, I would add a few embellishments, just to make it more true than it was • The last thing to disappear down the hole was his hair • Even I could not work up the energy to save the cat • I was out of explanations • That's when we figured out extinction wasn't necessarily forever • As long as he lives • But the baby already knew things I did not • Etcetera • It was the last time I saw her • Dawn light blinded me • A black oily stinking mess • Each gesture a way of enduring the pain • We must work with what we have • Try not to look • Below deck was where I would meet my fate • Yes, it was worth it • It wasn't my fault, the police report proved that • Murphy out • It was my only concession to conventional behavior • The prospect of love felt like a cheat • I would absorb the replacement cost • As though the inertia of the world was trying to find some place to call home • In the end, always, royalty will look after its own • No one but Manfred thought it was funny • The trudge up the road was more wearying than usual • We all did • And then there was the awful smell of the dead man, permeating everything, working its way into my soul, as though I needed something to make me feel worse than I already did • It felt good, but only for a few minutes • The wine had turned • When I cut the apple open I found it full of rot and worms • Her eyes rolled audibly • But in the end we all agreed the senator was well past his expiration date and would have to be terminated • It opened my eyes • Don't let it hurt you • No need for any more at this time • Most things don't last forever, but some, to my great surprise, do • Love ended it all • Our deal was the same as always: a pint of blood in exchange for a meal • Our family was not good at keeping secrets, but we kept that one for several generations, an astonishing and exemplary record that I was about to shatter • Do you know who I am? • "Believe me" • I longed for breath and the life it gave • "Mourn," said Lavinia, "then give thanks you knew them as long as you did" • The hall was dark and damp • The paint would not rub off my fingers for weeks after • The fort was a good thirty miles away, and with luck he would get there before running out of water and will • "It's on the house," he said • How many lives would I have to live? • It still bothers me that murderers can be forgiven • The baby, finally, was ours to keep • She still had hope in her heart • "Come on," he said, "let's get going" • But, the thing is, children grow up • "Yes," said Lily, "too bad" • Except me • We all slept in • We all died a little • "Talk to me," she said • The coffin was impossibly smooth and shiny • She kissed the top of her chemo-balded head • There were calls to make, but they could wait until morning • The tiger would be the first to go • And the lies were so banal and unnecessary • The invisibles returned later that day • I picked up the fork in the road • I never wanted a happy ending • I gave the medal to my daughter • The light was solid, like a cake • "It's all about the Flip" • She promised • And the queen was the prime suspect in the king's murder, but no one dared say it out loud • Snow doesn't fall on buried people, living or dead • The birdseed had spilled onto the ground

• Cheap whiskey is the best whiskey • So many words • And I think the best advice I ever got was to stop dreaming, or hoping, or believing • *I wonder what I lost that time,* she thinks • I saw her • I stood in front of the door fumbling for my keys • She was from Earth, after all • We moved together, without deciding, toward the bedroom • It didn't mean the same thing to me • They never did count all the ballots • Not a whimper or a bang, but more of a sizzle • Alone • I lowered my head and murmured a short soft prayer • I decided I would tell my daughter the whole story, everything from start to finish • I worked slowly, draping the coffin in an unfamiliar flag • I never trusted him • Heaven was never so boring • The invigorating and intoxicating smell of unburned coal • It was many years before their story was lost to memory • We didn't want to hurt anyone • The statue was made of marble • That was the meaning of her life • She placed the bowl on the table in the backyard where it would be flooded by sunlight • It was my turn to stay up all night • Even natural hearts need maintenance • We shared a warm glow • He waited for a long time for her reply • I put my ear close to her mouth, hoping for some last bit of wisdom • She was born with everything she needed • *C'est la vie* • Luna Colony would have to get along without me • So terribly lonely and afraid • They were all intent on witnessing the destruction • Columbus Day had its problems after that • Then it didn't seem so strange • But I had to throw that table out after all that had happened • Neptune rose, shedding sheets of water and seaweed as he turned on the craft, full of fury • My song, always my song • Yes, of course we did • He didn't want to hear about my operation, but I described it in detail anyway • He had no resistance left in him • She called me Grandma • The sun, still hot and bright, blazed above them and glinted off the Columbia into their eyes as they retraced their journey along the river back to the house • It was a spectacle not to be missed • A perfect night in Calcutta • I cried and no one thought to comfort me • Whenever we went to see my father in prison that year, we all got dressed in our nicest clothes, like we were going to church • In any case, and it pains me to say this, he will not be missed • I spent the night comforting the dog • Instead of opening the letter, I tore it into pieces and left it in the trash can at the post office • After a while I pulled away, or tried to, but he wouldn't let me and it felt good to have him clutching at me and I looked up to see Mom and Dad standing in the doorway, the most puzzled look on their faces you could imagine, and I just smiled at them and they tried to smile back but I don't know to this day if they really understood what had happened • I made it my own • We ended it • The births were unremarkable, thank goodness • Violets don't feel pain • The drink remained on the table, untasted and untouched • It still seems odd, even bizarre, and maybe impossible, that *zero* was something that had to be discovered • Then I leave him in the house and go tend to the horses in the barn • But no one wants to hear that story anymore • We passed roadkill after roadkill and Gerry just accepted it like it was normal • He had gotten his wish • Turned out, it was not a good day to die, not by a long shot • The fur was clearly from a wolf • They altered their world that day, and this time it lasted a little bit longer for both of them • Like a good soldier, I kept my mouth shut, and like a good soldier, I was rewarded with a sour taste on my tongue, and a bitter blow to my heart • The clock face reminded me of Walter • The last thing to know was about her lipstick • Nothing left for me to do in Juarez • I served the roast anyway • Because awarding a medal of valor to a robot is wrong • She signed her name and slid the contract across the table to the somber mediator who looked as though his sleep had been spoiled • Dinner was simultaneously awkward and glorious • "Stay down" • The bird angled its body left and took up a trajectory that would end at Eileen's forehead • A stain on history, no doubt, but one that propaganda would easily wash away • He hung the coat in the closet • That she chose to pose nude is no business of mine or yours • I loved that stupid cat • Not a good day to be from Io • And that's how *justice* can be a dirty word • Up the hill • A new dawn for a new nation • Starving actors are all alike • So many of them • "Hey," I say, "how did you get in here?" • My father's uniform was there, wrapped in tissue, nestled in a cardboard box • A roving band of artists is what we, absurdly, became • The hands burned bloody and black, as though the monsters of his dreams had manifested on the ends of his arms • We escaped just in time, as our country was then relegated to the imaginal realms, and we would have been forever lost with it • The sound of the creek remained, clean and sharp like the edge of a blade • It was up to me to inform the widow • The pain in his left arm • An icicle dagger ended the charade • I learned to dance • It would be an impossible job • Can I do it? • The soup needed more salt • She sits on the stone façade and talks to the guitar player who has finished strumming for now • The doctor says I won't even notice the loss after a while • His meals, it turned out, were quite literally *to die for* • She offered Brock her water bottle, but he refused, knowing it would be wasted • Being territorial does have its benefits • The extra week, this time, did not help • I purposely stabbed my finger on a cactus thorn • Water always helps • It was going to make an excellent story for page one • Rocks never felt so light • He never wanted to live in fear • The wine was all we found • Skin almost metallic • I tried to snatch the letter back from the fire, but it was already in flames • "Or maybe," he said, "he's still alive" • Venus had its attractions, I will admit, but in the end I had to sell the planet back to the syndicate, even though it was at a loss • But my craft became secondary and slipped away once the press dubbed me "the unlikely sex symbol" • Emotion is for weaklings • Phantom limbs everywhere • The awful image of her on the throne • Nature has a greater capacity for boredom than we do • Goodbye and good luck, Zap • The wind had hope in its soul • His evasions would not protect him forever • And then he touched his forehead for an instant, turned, and walked away • I would never tell him the truth • I carried the blame for Derrick • It was the land all along, right from the beginning • "Yes," said Rita, "you can come with us" • And anyway, looking back was always a loser's game • "This way," said Debbie • I began preparing the sauce • The vending machine refused to give up the candy bar again, but this time I didn't fight it • So many winters • Behind me the fat woman gleamed like a jewel in the sun and I loved her like I loved myself and I worked diligently, completing her family album there on the rock overlooking the eternal river, flowing past me like blood pushed by a stout heart • Really ugly socks • I never believed any of it until then • Never taste the flesh of your enemy, much less your friend • Her ashes in a paper maché house • Such pretty eyes, I thought • Best Thanksgiving ever • "You will have to convince me of that" • It was my shirt but it looked better on him, that I could not deny • All the ways of death settled in around her, like birds alighting on branches • She dropped the checkered flag and it flapped wildly against the wind generated by a dozen roaring race cars • I dropped the hammer on the chalk, making it explode into dust and crumbly bits that I would have to clean up later • A small tuft of fur • Four legs instead of two turned out to be a workable arrangement • An irregular coastline promises eternal peril • It wasn't worth the time • "You heard about my father's death?" I asked • I pulled branches off trees and arranged them on the frame of the lean-to and made a rudimentary bed beneath the branches and settled in just as night fell and the terror began to wake from its slumber • I directed him to the bottom drawer, where I had stowed my weapon earlier that year • My cat never once brought me a dead rodent • The picture showed my mother as a young woman, 60 years ago, full of wary life, ready to meet her fate • It was filled with alien babies • The voice on my phone told me to turn left at Morrison and continue on to I-84 and east to Twin Falls, which is what I did • The eruption of pain • The transformation would take years, but Kaylee had always been a patient person and would remain so for decades to come • She sang the only song she had left • A summing up was in order • It was all acceptable • All judgements, I decided, come in a rush • Except maybe me • That's all I'm saying • Remember your history, please, all of you • I handed the mic to the prisoner and the room went silent • She was a doctor, after all • Then as the day slipped into memory, the coyotes began their chorus of yips, sending shivers down my spine and bringing a tear to my eye • I raised my hand, then my voice, and finally my ire • Not a single one of us could remember • "You don't know me at all," said the bear • Turned out I should have suspected him all along • But the sea gave me no comfort • So I returned • "Do you want to go look for it?" • I wasn't made for funerals and did not attend Jade's • I never would again • With tentative hope, we pulled back the curtain • We kept watch while the children, and then the elders, drank from the pool • But being alone for so long meant nothing to him • She could imagine the heavens opening up in the same way • Completely unequal to the task • We had to stop after that • I climbed the stairs slowly • I was prepared to wait all night and into the morning • The silence between us • I dropped the gift onto the dirt of a potted plant and kept walking • So many • And that's how the world grew from a single bean • They didn't want to call it the promised land, despite all the assurances that it was easily the closest anyone would come to paradise • A scene like that, laid out in all its gory detail, never leaves you • Intelligence is, after all, a curse • And that's the point of having money • No more messages coming through the pipes • He always was a bit of an asshole • Dr Hanes smiled and smiled, her teeth shining like rows of lights, and she extended her hand and just kept walking toward Gibson • He spelled out his name, letter by letter, in a slow and soothing cadence • I put out the light and waited • You don't need light for enlightenment • I told him that everyone's getting older all the time but that did not comfort him one bit • I turned, in my doddering years, to making wigs • Lucky guy • Wishes are a waste of time • She placed her daughter's diary in the cornerstone of the half-finished building in the pre-dawn darkness before the construction crew arrived for their day's work • It was about three feet tall • He mutters something about how 68 years old is not a kid anymore • Bigfoot bid me goodbye and I never saw her again • The rock was palm-filling, hefty, and my only remaining connection to the old country • The bug in her hair was iridescent and lovely, like a jewel floating on a piece of black velvet • No one loved the creature after that, except Gregory • Made it seem like he knew what he was talking about when I knew he did not • Deep hoof-prints holding little pools of water • The freedom to choose • Awful patches of white fuzzy mold dotted his cheeks and ears • She bent her head to his chest • He stepped outside and began his search • I stood up and told her I was the missing link • After the trial, I bribed the evidence keeper for the murder weapon, which now sits on the mantle next to the picture of my father • Then why live? • Be dead if you need to be • No one saw it coming • Between the posts a sense of what was to come • He had his hands over his head, like a criminal • I went to the prison to visit my father four times that first year, then never again • All thanks had to go to the assassins and their mothers • She accepted his gift with slightly downturned eyes • I dabbed my sleeve in the king's blood • The road bed was just visible through the mist that wrapped the bridge in a gauzy fog • I never missed the wedding ring, not once • The dude sang all night • I ate all my greens • The carpet cleaner • Memories sting • I am no myth, no matter what your legends say • No one was coming to save us • So many reasons to die, all of them compelling • The junk drawer spilled its secrets onto the floor • The whale tasted like nothing he had ever experienced before • The dimming of the stars had begun • Georgette was certain • She laid the ruler against his cheek, held it there for a second, then wrote down the length of his scar in her notebook • Always there was his looking and looking, always looking • He had no right except the right a bully claims for himself • She left it on the desk to be mailed the next day • "Would you care to come join us?" • Thank you thank you thank you thank you • It didn't matter to me, or to anyone else in the room • It was open to the elements • He never bothered me again • But love is a language unknown to many and untranslatable for many more • Yeah, I said, for now • I call it the boomtown blues • I was then content to let events unfold at their own pace • Words didn't matter at that moment • She never asked me again • A picture of no consequence that still sold for three millions dollars • I raised a toast to my husband's killer • No other option, not anymore • There were worse things possible • Never kept a snake in the house after that • We agreed to the deal with a limp handshake • She wavered between hugging him and slugging him • I had no interest in his confession, but I could not stop his words • It looked uneasy, slightly out of place, like a ball bearing among marbles • Nights were made for silence • I watched the leaves go from green to red • The price was only five dollars • I took the script from her, even though I knew I would never even turn the first page, much less read any of it • "Hi, I'm Belle Z. Bub" • The whole town, every last one of us, was dancing wildly, as though spending our last ounce of energy • When the stories end, there's nothing left • They liked the feeling of a sky over their heads • For Elma there was no usual • The worst thing, by far, were all the bodies • Not fair, though, to blame the river • He bought two tickets • I patted the car twice, then saluted it and turned away, tears stinging my eyes • His response infuriated me, but I chose to display humility and love as much as I was able • You could say I had become a terrible person • There were numerous reports to read, as always, and then a strategy meeting with her cabinet • It is a land unknown to all but a few, and those few live only in torment from the knowing • They said I had to choose a door, which is why I chose the window instead • But he never believed me • Tears shared but hopes shielded from each other • And trees do weep, no matter what you've heard • No one but Rick would see it that way • I closed the door on him • At quitting time Ed's boss clapped him on the back and complimented him on his thorough efficiency • The flames • I don't think we are capable • I will then praise the lord • This time I believed him • Only what I draw is important • "I told you this would be a short visit" • He did not take his beating likc a man • I can always say I was part of the team that saved Neptune • But nothing happens without a stable supply route • I let the window snap shut • Antarctica will rip you open • For those who find such a stance comforting, there is nothing wrong with a pinch of gullibility • I bought the gun • That house had always been my sanctuary • You could call it a slow road to peace • Reincarnation is a scam • My loyalty had its limits • I worked feverishly to extinguish the voices of all those ghosts, and mostly succeeded • All those periods and commas stung me, and some drew blood • I made sure of that • No one saw it but me • The sunset was the worst cliché imaginable, but it was real, which made it even more ridiculous • You see the spot on the wall and you step closer to trace out its contours with your fingertip and nothing else matters at that moment • But I could not iron out any of the wrinkles, no matter how much I tried • But the tattoo, unnervingly, would not allow itself, under any circumstances, to be removed • Reader, I divorced him • Like a grown up • She would find a way • Never enough • If he ever finds out I'm not a holo, I'll lose his contract for sure • Don't try to understand them • Still hear the dying sounds of the ship breaking up as it sank • This did not turn out as I had hoped • But they would not listen • We clasped hands and ran for all we were worth • We ate as we always did: quickly, furtively, like the world might kill us, which, one day, and maybe soon, it will • Such precision of thought and action • Beyond the shops, the tower • *Earl* does have a satisfyingly noble ring to it • But I think he knew that was a story for another day • The brook flowed like snakeskin • The trees swayed in the wind • When they reached the park entrance they parted as strangers • No need to fear the future as it never comes and will always remain the future • Divorce was its own revelation • This has been my life • It took me three days to polish all the silver • It was not long before the vultures began wheeling overhead, circling the faintest of odors • "That would be nice," she said, as though her voice was a piece of jewelry she had lost many years ago and had only just recovered from the dust behind a couch in a corner of the room • I shave my beard off the next morning • No music in his voice • Nothing could then induce me to return to the alehouse • I asked my son to fetch me her father • The blood turned the rag red and ugly • My house swallowed everything whole • Wishes help no one • She knew she would catch the jar • Always begin fishing before dawn • His question was always the same: Why own anything? • "Not my fight" • Caroline found the ribbon in the trash can • Fighting the inevitable was my destiny, after all • He touches my shoulder but I shake him away • Not my job to make things better for him • We came to the new country and found it was different than we had expected • Nothing remained of the city except the church • Within a few minutes it had soared out of sight • I worked hard to forget him, but I never succeeded • Don't stop me, especially if you've heard this story before • But my street days didn't last • The coin rose high, as though carried by a water fountain, and glinted with sunlight as it fell onto his open palm • "You have your God, I have my bottle" • The documents were all sealed, not to be made public until everyone involved was dead at least fifty years • The gap between us felt smaller than it had ever been before • The paint, the faded paint • The network was at rest again • I never folded another crane in my life • The frozen ground would not yield to my shovel • The light reflected off the wall of the trailer and illuminated his eyes so they glowed in the darkness with a touch of magic to them • The infuriating silence of men • I did believe the years were going to be kind to her • His cat never liked me • Because all I wanted was everything • Religion had too many masks • I tore off my halo, shed my wings, donned my humility, descended to the Earth, and walked among my people • Never in our time • Too late, too late • Embarrassed, he tried to hide the motion by leaning back solidly • And that, my dears, is how I became princess of this court • Tears stung my eyes as I cut the rope to release his body • She saw it was a bit of wrapping from the birthday present • But that never happened • I paid for his passage • But justice turns to vengeance if you stay at this work for too long, and I was way past my sell-by date • Every journey ends with a final step • He would have preferred to abstain from voting • The storm, when it came, proved to be much less than it could have been • I stopped the howls the only way I knew how • She was desert-born • The third kitten would not stop its mewling • Her voice the exact replica of my mother's • But why would I have expected any different from a thief like Julie? • I turned off the light • Hide your money, always • All was peaceful and quiet and hidden from view • John blew smoke into the air as he watched them care for his boat • Not my fault life was good for me • It was all going to change • I won't forget • But beauty begins before bedlam • The tiny house had a body in it that was dead • They were a joy to see • I did savor the moment • Skulls, when all is said and done, are little more than clichés anyway • And pet ownership gives you the right to decide how to terminate a life • I put her on the bus to Edmonton • Fear is always there, a nasty friend you can't remove from your life • No light left • Finally, no secrets • The memory like a scar that changes, even heals, but never completely disappears • I pulled the bandage off and examined the wound, which was closed up, but still precarious • The coffee was weak • The threads of light through the slats • That particular bridge was painted an incongruous bright red • I loaded the shotgun and sat in a chair directly in front of the back door and I waited • No light, no light, no way, no how • Turns out, it actually *was* my circus *and* my monkeys • He carefully moved the belt off his shoulder and maneuvered it so his image remained askew and over the bed and with his own odd angel and twin looking on him, he stretched out on the bed and was quickly asleep • Everyone knew • I chose the snake • Best thing that ever happened to anyone • His blue tongue and red teeth • Each wave was different from the one before, but also maddeningly the same • No one believed I not only allowed my kidnapping, but also welcomed it • "I may return and I may not" • Stop me if you haven't heard this before • He bid the fairy goodbye, and she fluttered her wings before him, bowed in midair, and flew away • The statue fell, in slow motion it seemed, and crumbled to dust on the street • and no I said no I won't No • And the dozens of orphans, waiting for the world to come back • His hug crushed me • My fear was contagious, I could see that • But I suppose all of this was inevitable once the ghosts hijacked the time machine • I was to have no access at all • The crane snapped and creaked and screeched as it tumbled over and fell to the street below • The thing is, everything God makes will die • The bridge had iced up and looked like a shimmery ghost in the early morning fog • A good time to turn the calendar page • "Exactly," he said to her • I still carry Flatland with me • I couldn't watch • Everyone in the house was sick that month • "Hello" • For his last meal he chose a simple bowl of rice with vegetables and a few morsels of pork • That was how it went that week in Montreal • Home was always an ugly word after that • It was a winning lottery ticket, but I told her it was a bust and tore it into pieces • She tried for many years, but in the end she could not forgive him • The street people thanked me • Whether death is the ultimate cruelty or the ultimate glory remains unknown • They pulled me out of the water and nursed me back to health, all the while telling me I was most likely going to die and there was nothing they could do about it but they were going to try as hard as they could to keep me alive • Cheering crowds, lots of them, enough to scare me into silence • In the event, with chaos roiling around them, he calmly prepared the last meal any of them would ever eat • He closed each door and went downstairs to be with Ramona • She was considerate enough to wait for her parents to die before she hanged herself • The tie, especially, was ill-fitting • Such strong lungs from one so small • Because my question was never "why?" or "when?" or even "who?" but rather: "how much?" • No answer to his questions • Death left his black robe at my dry cleaning shop, hoping I could get the blood stains out, but I never could, not ever • Never wondered why • She would be a free spirit then, and nothing could bring her down to Earth • My last words to her I have already forgotten • I cannot convey the pain it caused me • Leaves like snow • She furrowed her eyebrows, puzzled by his stern tone • It would never be soon enough • His laughter was less than appropriate but we all chose to ignore it • Toothy grins are creepy anyway, don't you think? • I cried as I watched the bots dismantle my starship • They had their own secret language, and it was ugly • That's why I always sing in graveyards • It was just a piece of land • "I was there" • He woke to fire • From the direction of the city of golden light they heard the unmistakable sound of a soothing, steady rain • That's when I dropped from the tree to the ground, poised to spring • It was nothing more than bad weather • I set the soup to simmer and ignored the pot for the rest of the afternoon • The blanket was thin and frayed but I was still grateful for it • It was forever after known as the Tacoma Terror • The fox spoke, which startled everyone but Tom • I didn't stay for the execution • "For Texas!" • The comfort of it all • They were savages, created in my image • Just one more time • "Leave it" • Her smile faded quickly • It's the only form of time travel we will ever have • The sound of laughter spilled out of the bar into the street, where we listened, quietly, until it dissipated and we were left in silence that gave comfort to no one • Shadows highlighted her features • But you know all of that by now, or should • He fell through the floor to the basement where he suffered a broken leg and a concussion • Never did care for thirsty wood • I now had a stolen painting in my possession, and no idea what to do with it •

I saw the way clear to the end of my days • My turn came before I knew it • The mutants, all of them, thanked me for the con • "Come on, let's go," he said • We named the town Gamble • The rain was black, oily, and unceasing • "The usual," I said • Turtle races, after all, are slow affairs • The promise of nuclear fusion • The fading twilight accentuated his face with enticing shadows • So much blood • Marina murmured her assent • Then I lift my hand and make a spiral in the air and wish only good thoughts for everyone and everything in the world • I will always appreciate childish things • The protesters were my people, after all • Animals leave pieces of themselves behind, and they don't care, they have no emotional attachment that I have ever seen • You don't like it, but you end up putting a price on life • Go to the moon, then, and see what they have to offer you, because I think Earth is done with you • Dead birds littered the ground under the window • Such sweet light • And the dog, trapped in the hot car and barking like a thing possessed, did not move me or my children • Within five minutes the table was empty • So many names • Nothing pleased him more • No more sleeping on park benches • I then retired from the bakery and took up the manufacture of candlesticks • They both knew winter was the worst season for love, but neither of them cared • They were Halifax Knights • I was still getting used to seeing the truth • Not in this life, anyway • "Do you even know what a zoo is?" • We descended along the creek, walking until after dark, something we knew we shouldn't do • The fishing tomorrow promised to be spectacular • She was my favorite child • Next time • The playoffs, after all, is where hope goes to die • The aria defeated me, as it always did • No one should get away with what he did and I made sure, this time, that he didn't • She was my guide and mentor and I still miss her terribly • That was the night everything changed • It was as though a million earthquakes went off at once • Heavier than I expected • Such a terrible ending • A creature made of weeds • I left the tickets on the table • They held up traffic for hours • A dozen gold nails • The razor was 12 feet long • But when did my eyes turn purple? • Once she had seen the dragons hatch • But the shaking did not stop, mine or the ground's • It was his masterpiece • Truth resided between his moans • The mirror shattered • I made the coffee • It always feels good to be inconvenient • I was tired of cutting hair • As a tribute, I trimmed the hedge to look like her • It was so close • Stay well and happy, that's all • And anyway, what good is a house with no mirrors? • I always liked his advice, but I never followed it • His hair looked better then • So if anyone ever asks, you can tell them *that* is how you get away with murder • It might have been his last coherent thought • It does make me wonder • But he wasn't supposed to make any mistakes, that was our deal • I changed my name • Take them away, take them far, far away • He went from cage to cage, opening each in turn, and letting the occupants out to fly free • The park was too green, too manicured, and too empty • The sea was still there • Can't blame God for that • Human, as best I could determine • They were extra graves • It was my ode to darkness • Just don't call him a dream master • But the darkness did not allow easy identification • The future belongs to everyone • They were young, and thought they always would be • I buried him near the orchard • He never told me • Because none of it, *none of it*, mattered anymore • She looked at the ceiling where Vonda's eyes stared, but saw nothing • The tree cracked and groaned as it fell • That was the way she wanted it • It told her she didn't have to *do* anything to deserve love • Forget the past and the future • A gloppy green ocean, covered with vegetation, sloshed out to the horizon • There was that question again, coming back to Verol as he remembered yesterday • As he followed Mr McCabe to the road he didn't notice the stars shining above him • It took them less than a day to paint the entire house • That's when the terror began • The light switch was sticky with blood • It was very good flying weather all that day • He didn't think it was too much to ask • The ladder was perfect • Not something anyone should see • The key would not fit the lock • Most people can't handle the fact that murderers escape justice every day • Nothing but static on all TV and radio channels, and nothing but fear in all my hearts • He climbed up the steps, being careful to avoid the one that emitted a squeak of true annoyance at the slightest pressure • And when presented with his plate, Ivan gamely pretended he was okay with fried snake • We finally found both bodies in the ravine as the sun was rising • I've been told that you don't have to live happily *ever* after to have a happy life • They dined on moldy bread and questionable water while the shells burst around them • There was no reason to love him • And, really, murder was the least of it • Her strong calloused hands • Four days later, we staggered out of the desert to our new lives • Life will still be tough, but we can face it together • The eggs were rotten • Still shaking my head at the mere *existence* of a working pay phone, I dropped four quarters into the slot at the top and listened with rapt awe to the dial tone • No one was at fault, no matter what the district attorney believed • I didn't know the soldier, but I recognized him • The volume fit comfortably in my hand, but its contents rested uneasily in my mind • It was sobering to think of him as my ancestor • He waited • Just as my mother had done in her day • My heart just dies, like it's a stomped-on bug • Desire kills • The tiger's paw still had claws • I had forgotten, but I guess my heart remembered • There will always be time • They still live in my nightmares, which occur at least once a night • He had my support • Lies we tell to and about ourselves are the most enticing and also the most damaging • God help me, I still believe he deserved all the pain he got • Then it is nothing but sleep that you want • After a long time, maybe a half hour, with the sun finally peeking over the mountains and bathing the house with lovely light, Marcy and I cleaned up Lillian's tipped over plants • I held him at the throat until he stopped thrashing • Home was just around the next curve in the trail • Like dolphins in the rain • We waited in silence • They covered her • The landlord did not have the last laugh • People don't rise from the dead unless they are truly enraged by some slight • I flipped the OPEN sign around and locked the door against the town • I guess there are worse things than being exiled from your home planet • He could not remember the rip not being there, so much had it become a part of the shirt • My son ate in peace • The carcass remained at the edge of the property all through that cold damp autumn • If he said "Pain is an illusion," one more time, I was going to slug him, hard, then ask him if his illusion felt bad • That would have to be the next thing he did • I held her for several minutes • I hit the wall some time around the fifteenth mile • His wedding band • But I will not complain about Emmett, now or ever in the future • I bid the aliens good bye and told them never to return • I told him to stop telling stories until he learned how • He showed what he truly was • A simple kiss was always best • Spring is largely overrated anyway • I feel my hair engulf the world • We were okay with rain • The flag never looked more right than when we flew it upside down that morning • There was no other choice • You have come to the end • We found the vein of quartz on the third day • He tried to keep his thoughts to himself, but they were written all over his face • In those days, that was how we acquired husbands • It was a worn thing, barely better than rags sewn together, but I told him I would mend it for him and he was so grateful it embarrassed us both, or should have • He made sure no one saw him in that country ever again • I made her a sandwich • Always best to redeem your coupons as soon as possible • Prolly not the way anybodies should be talkin • It's a free country, for the moment • I put one hoof in front of the other and began searching for my friends • The mountain told us • She never learned that movies aren't like life • I never thought it would come true • He filled the revolver with bullets, drew in what was to be one of his last breaths, and stepped out of the corner into the light • I crawled out of the trench with some difficulty and rose unsteadily to my feet and turned to the road and waited for a car to pass by that I could flag down and ask for help • The dancing went on all night • We spent the rest of the day walking backward together • "I think I'll sleep this one out," he said • I pushed the door open and it shattered, sending glass shards onto my wrists and shoes • The wax melted • The dust was a strange pink color • I boarded the bus and took a seat and thought about what I was going to tell Lila when I got home • I hoped my new identity would flourish in Oregon • The hut erupted into flames and the screaming began • "We don't know if we made the right decision, and we don't know if we are up to the task" • The painting remained ugly • He fought valiantly against my strength, which only made me respect him even more and gave me a pang of regret for killing him • Character was the best kind of assassination, everyone knew that • Fist bumps all around • I always thought peace was overrated, and, in any case, as the previous pages have shown, not my strong suit • The ship carried her away • That steady droning hum • Never did go to see her, and never regretted not doing so • Graves don't usually speak so eloquently • She decided it was best if vampires refrained from being detectives • Decay happens quickly • The artifacts of war remain • She was a stranger, but that did not prevent Hattie from comforting her as she died • The song lingered in the air and in her ears until silence enveloped all • The last thing to go was phone service, right after they cut off my electricity • I explained it was the lateness of the hour • So many feathers everywhere • In the fall, his skin turned shades of yellow and red, mimicking the trees around him, and fascinating all the children in the neighborhood who could not stop staring at him • He pulled the rabbit out of his hat • She placed a SOLD card next to Lena's sculpture • Abdication had its points • But I never learned • The dogs, instinctively, formed a pack and began to hunt • The end of the day coincided with the start of our affair • A flock of men and women with wings shadowed the sky • I never told anyone that my weeks had eight days instead of seven • The ghost saw me, I am sure of it • He hated me because I had an easy life • No words were necessary • The task of finding and dispatching the traitor was one I was going to relish • It was years before I regretted any of what I did that week • Trying to find a way back to what I had been • You could call it a house, but that would be a stretch • But I could accept it as a proper punishment • The only difference was that my name wasn't Moses • Open wide • The sound of bones breaking • No, never • I think I've already told you the Statue of Liberty always makes me laugh • I suppose I was an unreliable narrator • Wasn't her time • No need to get all complicated about it • Her apology took a long time to parse and understand • Ha ha ha ha ha ha ha ha ha • He spent the rest of the weekend figuring out what he would tell Hayley on Monday morning • He said he wanted to marry me, which just made me laugh so hard I cried • I listened as he described his own drowning • "Stop it, Poppa, please" • It was the season I made two dozen bad calls, which is why it was my last season of umpiring • Believe what I say, but don't embarrass me by telling anyone else • I saw no recognition in her eyes • We've got a lot to learn • The tribe had done nothing for me • That's when I let God go from my life • The wind that year brought only misery • "Sounds pretty stupid," he said • He should have died then • Imagination always falls short • The baby shoes • "Ready?" • And then, much to my surprise, I thanked him • Some birds had built a nest on the balcony • The people, all with bright fiery eyes, pressed closer to the child, and no easy outcome seemed possible • Darkness was always welcome, and always would be, at least in my town • Her look • My testimony took three full days • We would all remember that day • We culled the weak ones, just like nature herself does every day • Sacrifice usually suffices in these circumstances • All the evil in the world • The envelope from Harvard was thick enough to be an acceptance, but I did not open it for a long time • I'll leave those kinds of judgments to the historians • "It's me," I said • We got out just in time • Not like this • A gray mass, hovering, trembling, and sinister • The deception was complete • In the end I didn't mind the lies • Her feelings about the estate were well known, after all • We walked out of the grocery store with my hand in hers, she walking briskly to the car, me twisting around to catch just one more glimpse of the craft that gave me my first taste of freedom • Haven't had a good night's sleep since then • A gold coin, unblemished, and shinier than the sun • No one can say if it will matter • But I see the future, remember? • So am I • I could not know, at that moment, if I would regret what I did • I packed as quickly as I could • Desire rules • The crisis was over but the damage had just begun • History would be a harsh judge of his actions • A pessimist always knows • That dog was, and always would be, nothing but trouble • He decided everything else should follow pretty easily • The lives of the animals • I didn't dare ask his opinion, and now I regret my loss of nerve • The noose was more comfortable than a tie • Balconies on tall buildings are nothing but suicide invitations • That's what power does to a person • The pigeons rose with a flutter and fuss of wings, beating the air and inadvertently distracting me from the melancholy in my heart • The rope burns lingered on my wrist and ankles for several days • If physics teaches us anything it is that there are no separate ways • "Now, everyone, take a deep breath" • It was the junior senator from Montana • Stopping the campaign was out of the question • The coppery taste of the air after a party • The award felt heavy and ridiculous in my hands • "Don't let the ice fool you" • The city beckoned • I had no hope for the message, but I sent it through the ether anyway • I turned away from the body, even as I knew the gesture was proof of my privilege • I would have to wait until she died • As it turned out, I was patient zero • But I have always believed that death improves the ability of most any musician • I had to • Ordinary lives lived by ordinary people • I ate the soup • It had seen better days, but it would do • Whenever I passed the library • Like an old man • I turned the key and the car sputtered and huffed and shook, but did not start • No one expects to see a dog with a wooden leg • You ever try to cash a check signed by God? • Those thoughts did me no good at all • The sticky, sickening trail of a slug • Only then did I call the police • Spring *is* the season with the most promise, but it holds the seeds of disappointment as well • She will look for you • That's what powerlessness does to a person • Don't ever serve me green beans • There were 184 bullet holes in the walls that took two weeks to repair • The king and the queen begged for mercy that was not in him • It was easily the best wheelchair I ever had • I tried to revive the feeling, but it was gone • I had lost a whole day • She had a right to know her son was a vampire •

The glory of that day would not be diminished • Praise be • "Hold it up," she said, "so the birds can see it" • Anyway, my shipmates, for the most part, deserved to die • My grandmother said it was her horse and no one argued with her on that point • Her animal nature never left her • Some days things just work out and it doesn't pay to question why • I held up my arm, now handless, for him to see and be shocked by • She calculated she had a good twenty years left • Over the garage • I saw with delight that she had used my recipe after all • Blythe worried all the same • He was a bad man • I found the dog on the street and made sure it was ready for space flight, but didn't know it was going to die in space • The lights flickered • Snap! • There is always something wrong, somewhere, for someone • They remember the meteor • The limits of our knowledge • The smoke rose, as smoke generally does, until it disappeared in the wind • A pink angora sweater, freshly laundered, and nestled in a satiny white box interleaved with pale blue tissue paper • When we got there a glass float, like a glistening egg, lay half-buried in the sand • He was my friend • It was only one shoe, true, but it fit him perfectly and he kept it and wore it for the next three years • His disgusting odor was, astonishingly, a welcome comfort to her in those final days • The meal had no taste • Turns out, once all the dust had settled, that he operated under no less than 12 aliases • I saw the signature on the painting was my own • At least it was, even in all its dreariness and squalor, a room of my own • You gots to bend tings to makes a civilization that work for everones • Learn it fast, for everyone's sake • And the light was exactly what I expected • He held the moment as one might hold one's breath • I could not make my mouth smile • Never trust a talking dog • "Yes," she said, "I am your mother" • I am warmed by their eternal and benevolent presence • Her healing hands • He was the last of his kind • My twin • The creases in her palm, she now saw, were a map of her country • We searched the area for another week, then had to admit defeat • The handle broke • Fear keeps us from many things • I held the picture up and my hand trembled with the effort • Too many beneficiaries and none of them the least bit grateful • And really, who'd a thunk it? • The medal felt too heavy on my chest • Sleep should hold you in its arms, after all • She rewrapped the baseball with the spare covers, sewing them tightly closed by hand, using the thick needle and the bright red thread • The rain streaked the sky • They were intruders, true, even criminals, murderous ones, but there was no need to make his last minutes in this realm anything but pleasant, so he asked them to put down their weapons for a brief interlude and join him in some tea and biscuits, so they could all get to know each other before the killing began • "Yes," he said, over and over, "yes yes yes yes yes" • So grateful for so much, most especially the ground, always there to meet my sole whenever I take a step • It wasn't my time • She put the car into gear—for the last time in her life—and shot forward hard enough to press her head against the seat back • That would have to be enough • It filled me with rage that she got her wish • See the result of your fun and games • I was glad it was my last case • He never shook the feeling that someone was hovering over him, trying to invade his thoughts • I think even the sky trembled a little • The marauders arrived as expected, and they did what was necessary to the victims that remained • We never left • The cave eventually tired of us • A calendar made of marshmallows • The terror would come later • They lingered for an instant—that seemed like an eternity—and then they were gone on the currents of air • No need to study anything else but the dead body • Silence, after all, was too much to expect • It was good to have a world of his own • Shadows never scared me until that night • His kindness was a sham • That moment, or the memory of it, has never left me • I would have to fix that rattle • Galapagos always eats its young • See how it is? • "No," said the fat man to his dog, "that is quite impossible" • All the words were there on the back of my tongue waiting to be flung into air • Forgiveness • It was all about economics • By and by • You can still go to the hall and see the body, if you are inclined to such gruesomeness • The symbol of light • I composed myself and put on my best expression • The drink tasted lousy • But no tears, please • A river of bullets, but none touched me • It was time for an end to fairy tales • Always best to allow the wind a clear path • His laugh, however, still grated on all my nerves • A heap of dirty clothes • But he had to make himself remember that magic is a scam and always will be • But giving up is a kind of victory as well • The crops were there, ripe and waiting, but none of the superstitious pickers would go into the fields, and, really, I didn't blame them one bit • "But this is our best chance and we have to try whatever we can" • No one wanted to go to the stars anymore, so none of us boarded the starship, and it lifted off without a human in any of the berths • His cough, for the first time, brought up a thick clot of blood • A spider, crawling across the picture, leaving no tracks • The shirt required numerous repairs and I worked on it for the next hour • The copier hummed and chattered and rolled out a blank sheet of paper • Every ending is a nail in a coffin • No one wanted that • The knife always scared me after that • He did get to see the blossoms one last time • They then referred to me that day, and every day afterward, as Andromeda • The script retained only one of my lines • We shook hands and never saw each other again • And I had some matters to attend to • Bob's door never did dilate • His sons were attentive and kind right up to the end • Every story, like every life, has an appropriate ending • Yes, these people all around me were my family • No one saw the humor except me • The clogged arteries, the flesh encased in fat, the soul smothered • "It did have its effects," I said • I marked the ballot and dropped it into the box • So many broken windows • Our home world receded to a dot behind us • They all, every last one of them, looked exactly like me • We got the kite flying and took turns holding onto the string for rest of the day • "Poke it," said Ralph, and before I could stop him, that's what he did • As if • It didn't stand for anything • Don't know why she thought life was ever going to be fair • The androids • They removed the tattoo from my forehead • But Elmore's hopes were always the highest • A Stradivarius, for goodness sake, stored for decades in this man's basement • He dropped Sid's head in the dumpster and barely gave him another thought • The thermometer that afternoon read 42 degrees, seriously celsius • "My name's Keith," he said, "and it means from an unknown place" • And what did I find inside the creature but an intricate and disconcerting assembly of gears, churning away in the cavity of its chest • Every house had at least one purple blood beetle, each one a guardian of hope • Can't be true • I lit the match and brought it to the tip of my cigarette • He looked dead and it took me some few minutes to finally make myself go over and check to make sure • The package arrived sooner than he expected • But for those left behind, no case is ever over • "This way," he said, "look this way please" • All of this happened on a night lit by a full moon • The portrait was underneath the landscape • I pulled back the closet door and told the girl inside everything was going to be okay • "I think we need to go to the sea," she said • Never promise anything to anyone if you want a life of ease • Then it was just the two of us, always together, keeping the world at bay • It was native blood • But it wuz jus like I tells the nurse: you don't wan ever to see any a doze tings cept maybe in your dreams times • He scheduled a return to the city as soon as his trip was over • No one should have to look at a starless sky • A thundering sound, killing everything • Good byes don't always hurt • I hope not • My collaborator was at the door • No one saw it but me • His last act of freedom was to resist the king • I dismissed the sensations • I remembered that the cleaner on Davis and Third was the best at discreetly removing blood stains • I learned marriage is an end as much as it is a beginning • She made a list of her secrets and studied them for longer than was healthy • I really wanted someone else's memory of the event, if only it was possible to achieve such a thing • He couldn't let himself get too close • Too late to decide not to have children • They saved my life, and I should have been grateful, but I would have preferred death • Swans don't have a song • There are phantoms everywhere, he said • So many wishes and none of them mine • I heard a dog howling • The kittens—there were so many of them!—rose up from their slumber and made a great wave of claws and teeth and advanced on poor Marty with unquenchable ferocity • I did recuse myself, just to be safe • And don't get me started on Alyssa • We found him curled up in the basement, clutching the gun close to his chest • His laugh, always his laugh, there on the edge of perception like a permanent light flash in my peripheral vision, forever mucking things up • My ferret's world • Always a reason for despair • One star won't cast a shadow, but a million will • Every day will feel like my last • I did see that my cape needed ironing • What he taught me should not be learned by anyone, anywhere, any time • And the wondering will soon be over • Don't ever grow up • Long, steady breaths • We ate generous helpings of the light • I noticed the cherry tree was just beginning to blossom • Failure is its own re-ward • The bugs take flight • "Doesn't it tell you something?" asked Renae • He was bleeding in three places and I held him until he died • No planet like it, ever • "In what order would you like your wishes granted?" • The feeling of doom and gloom and the slap of a broom • "Sit down," he said as he settled into his chair, "and let me tell you the whole sad story of my life" • See how it is? • I looked at him and he purposely did not look back, but I could see his sly smile and I knew he was feeling proud of what he had just done • The natural curve of the smooth rocks • No way to see her as innocent after that • We began the culling with a bloody prayer • Strength comes from many places • My father said • I saw it as a victory, the only one we would get that day • The cries of the child doomed us all • We leave the suits at home • Her alien qualities will forever keep her from assimilating • My gallon jar full of pennies • Sometimes I think it might be beneficial to bring back the custom of madhouses, if only for a select few of our fellow citizens • He was front and center in the picture • And little Viola said the prayer • The sea was the color of our quilt • The welcome heat we generated under the sheets • But in my dreams and wishes it is always what it shouldn't be • That's what it takes to win • We shared breakfast • Monday, always Monday • The visions were becoming more numerous • Revenge came later than he expected • Such difficult memories • I drained the glass, but it was not enough, not by a long shot • I spent the rest of the day practicing Chopin's Opus 25 Number 1, *The Aeolian Harp,* barely able to read the sheet music through my tears • I picked up my hammer and chisel and approached the slab with something akin to determination • It would take a lot more effort to understand the inmate's motives • They sang *Happy Birthday* with no enthusiasm • We spent a glorious evening together, talking about Slothin and her strange ways • The dirty plates turned my stomach • The violin, I don't mind saying, completely defeated me • "Don't you see that the jewels were fake all along?" • I'll miss you • Under your feet, always • The house was finally satisfied • I spent the rest of the afternoon scrubbing the graffiti off the side of the grain elevator • Gasping for air • They were always the most hungry right after waking up • The kid had the candy in his pocket, but I let him go • Desert air always includes the hope of moisture • Better a dead world than no world at all • The can of cat food went unopened • Even burning eyes can see • The windsock fluttered, then inflated with cold air coming down from the north in a sharp, shocking breeze • But I stood in the window awaiting his arrival, which never came • I went to my daughter • His thanks for my service was not worth the loss of my legs or the scars on my face • Never went back there • I agreed to bring the boy into my house • The doctor said I shouldn't even be on the planet anymore • It wasn't funny, though it should have been • The living persist • I painted the house • Not his fault, this time • Even now, with the end coming closer and closer by the second, it is difficult to decide who was right • The prettiest planet I had ever visited • Angels, he decided, had a lot to answer for • I explained the mutiny to the captain's wife with my head bent down the entire time • Given half a chance, literature *will* kill you • His calls were still unnerving • It was the start of something, but that something was small • I would never share her joy and optimism • My poor cat • I never cared for that word • My disappearance pleased no one and everyone • It painted the sky a deep red, deeper than any red I had ever seen • His cat liked the water, after all, and was always interested in a sea voyage to anywhere • His heart needed transplanting • I tore off the doll's head and threw it against the wall • I told him I would go to the car and retrieve it • The sheen of paradise never looked so tarnished • I fought the nausea and snapped the picture • The tune was easy, memorable, silly, and bigger than anyone could have hoped for • So easy to blame everyone • Over the next few years I watched the lake shrivel and dry up until it was just a mass of dried seaweed, maybe hoping to become a meadow • The spark-less ones, flowing past their own dreams • I brushed off the welcome mat and placed it in front of the door • Not as ordinary as one might think • Train stations always look their loneliest at night • It was, as the saying has it, under cover of darkness • The dog wouldn't stop barking • I took an icicle from the side of the house and gave it to Jessie • The delay proved to be entirely Ezra's fault • I dropped the file in the garbage can near the entrance to the newspaper building, knowing Jaqueline would find it there • My verbs, pulled out of the past, were the best for vanquishing the beasts • Cleaning up afterwards, before the police arrive, is always a desperate affair • After all, the car was unlocked, with the keys in plain view • We released Bander to the wild at the base of Sinclair Mountain and as she sauntered up the slope toward the pine trees in the distance, she did not hesitate or turn her head to us and we did not say *goodbye* or *farewell* or even *see you later* • My lemonade stand lay in ruins, crushed by the kids on the next block, who were going to pay for their transgression, believe me • But I did detect what I took to be a note of contempt in her eyes as I handed her the folded flag • Portraits always lie • I dropped the package and waited for his kiss • They turned it upside down and it all felt better • We turned the car around and headed to Boise • The best wine I ever tasted and only God to thank for it • The white fence bordering brown grass • Of what? • Take your time, my love, take your time • I spent the rest of the day, on into evening, fishing • I sat in the dark for a long time and didn't come out until the sun was long gone and the wind off the water filled my world with sharp smells and an icy cold • The realm of the elves beckoned and we were ready to answer the call • The weather hung above us like a framed picture • We were ready • They counted for something • It took some time, but eventually the haze cleared enough for me to see it was Georgina in the distance, waving her arms over her head like a windmill • No way to prove any of it • I avoided sleep, knowing the dead children would appear in my dreams • I spent the rest of the afternoon completing the report • Lemony green beans with garlic, crispy fried chicken, buttery mashed potatoes, and a nice lemon meringue pie for dessert • The foghorn marked the passing of a life • The sun rose before us and we crawled toward it at a stately ten miles per hour, all the while feeling the cool air of dawn against our cheeks • In the end he used a blade he himself had sharpened in the traditional manner, with oil and a stone • Never the robot's fault • She would not agree • We made popcorn and pretended we weren't interested in the execution, but we were, all of us, and we watched with rapt attention to the very end • I won't, not anymore • When the moment came I deliberately aimed away from the prisoner, to honor the memory of my father, who, against all common sense, remained a pacifist to his last day • The sky had its own agenda • The wizard, breathing his last, plunged the realm into a magic-less chaos that lasted longer than anyone's memory of him • Everyone knew • That's when I knew there was no chance • The plane's shadow darkened her face just as the world was insulted by the sound of tearing buildings and screaming citizens • He had that thought because he had never been a criminal and likely never would • *You are responsible for spreading this evil around the world, only you* • The horse was uneasy, which meant a storm was coming and I would have to take shelter • Pride turned out to be an ill-fitting garment • The soap never changed • Trouble the spirit • The wind brought so much into the square • The train did not look inviting at all • The Grand Canyon is one of those rare things that is *not* overrated • The package from Jenny was heftier than I expected • No explanation for some people • Her story was ugly and awkward but I pretended to like it • He took the same table he had had before, and waited • Suppose you don't exist • My way • "There, you see," said his uncle • I swear it was not my fault, any of it • I sat down and wrote her obituary • We were nine years old, newly married, and my mother told me I would not see my new husband for another 12 years, by which time both our empires would require our union to be pure and strong and loving • I will see the end, if I choose to • The vine, improbably, wound around the tree, cutting a bright green helix through the dry yellowing leaves • No one remembers her anymore • But the greatest discovery of all was that we could invent reality • But the ice, the ice, it kept melting • Then he said it again • The stars moved in meandering arcs, like fireflies in the night, and they stared, open-mouthed, waiting for the world to end • The blood-stained walls were an odd comfort to me that evening • A zombie nation must rise from the ashes • He had a little smear of paint, pink and bright, just below his ear • The coroner, always the coroner, no matter what the circumstances • They were all my mistakes • The blast made us all jump • No one saw her after that • She jumped out of the cake, like this was some kind of bachelor's party from 1948 • They moved slowly, as protocol suggested, and Mimi demanded • Malcolm's report did not mention the drugs • And her shrugs were as infuriating as they had ever been • He approached the package slowly, exercising all the caution he had in him • I had found the limits of our friendship • The string broke • The feathers only brought fear to his heart • He watched them criss-cross the blue sky, then grabbed his backpack, slung it over his shoulder, and began walking to school • But what she thought was a discarded blanket turned out to be the giant's shirt • I still hate caller ID • But he did not want to let him go, ever • The tap on the door was the unmistakable musical rat-a-tat-tat of the undertaker's assistant • The map was a lie, and it was my fault that I trusted it • Lots of thoughts like that one • His face displayed no features • "Next, please" • It also proved to everyone that I would take my dog over my children, always • Annette mirrored the knife's attitude and repose, waiting for words, always waiting • Dog hair covered the chair • They laughed in the bright sun and I remembered the music of my Liana which seemed to rise from the melting snow and cover the children with happiness and warmth and a kind of love that I knew would take me a long time to understand • But Tim, as I've mentioned, always was a picky eater • No one was ever more foolish or more alive • She bore the weight of both years and tears • I had achieved a level of comfort unprecedented in history • Some folks choose not to take lessons from any of their successes or failures • Emu feathers • Soup and a sandwich • I tried the trick of counting sheep, even though it felt absurd • But it was much too late for any of that • He told her the story of the encounter, in every detail, leaving nothing, even his own morally questionable actions, out of the narrative • The plane taxied out to the runway and after a short wait we were airborne just about the time I reached into my pocket and felt for the box cutter I had put there that morning • The strawberries were dotted with white furry spots of mold • The footsteps drew closer as we held our breaths • It was my mountain and no one else's • My hand did not feel like it was mine • Those days were the answer to everything • I burned our only map in the campfire, then planned how I was going to break the news to Colby when he woke up • A silence, then, like no other • No time left to be a child • Her work was just beginning • I saw, with horror, that it was my skin • He left her on the pier and boarded the ship that would be his home for the next year • *Almost* anything • I closed the eyes of the beast and turned to its tormentor with renewed fury • My face showed its shame • But I may lose my fight • So tired, always • It's what we always talk about, all the time • The devil's tail was a ropy thing, with that absurd arrow on the end, and a kind of hot lava oozing out of the opposite severed end, and it felt good to hold it high over my head and hear the cheers of my comrades in arms against evil • The body, clearly, was just at the beginning of the decaying process • Las Vegas knew • Snow was on its way, and it was already too late to prepare for it • "For your own good," she said • Even the rats could tell • I propped the door open, hoping he would find me • That was the last time I saw the president alive • I took only my weapon and my training to the village that day • No worlds left, only the refugees seeking some kind of comfort • I estimated we were only about 12 hours ahead of the mob, and losing ground quickly • The point of it all • A blood stain on the third step • We worked to fill the space • Her gaze would never be centered on his or anyone's face as she spoke • The rats feasted noisily that night • Hubert and I hiked for a while until we got to a stretch in the trail where the side sloped sharply down to jagged rocks some three hundred feet below, and I pushed him over the edge • Drowning helped • Roses wilt • His tale entertained them through the night with his robust telling, and no one regretted the sleep they lost • Invented languages usually disappointed me anyway • I ate the last one without asking anyone else at the table • Penelope wore a wig of horse hair • Her earring was missing • She made a whiskey swizzle for him • I stood outside the church and listened to the choir for several minutes • "I really don't know" • Not the sky's fault • It was our rule, after all: Do what needs doing, then deny and move on • The ground was hard, the shovel was small, and there was precious little sunlight left • It made no difference • Driving home, he decided to quit his job • Better to be alone anyway • We cut down trees, we cleared land, we built roads, we planted crops, we did all the things we would regret in the years to come • I killed the bottle, then threw it into the fireplace, making sure it shattered • And then she died, which, disconcertingly, changed nothing • "Why are you home so early?" • She really *really* needed to blow her nose • The burn remained on my arm, where he had put it, for the next decade, a reminder of our mutual loathing • Her first trip since the accident • Cutting down the gallows tree was the right thing to do, even though it killed the tree • With energy and determination the horses pounded the ground till they exhausted themselves • There is always a future, however bleak • Her face remains in my memory, distorted, perhaps, but still beautiful, always beautiful • Punishment was not my area, after all • He began dying that morning and kept it up for the next 12 years • That was something no one could be sure of • We made the world safe, but we didn't know for who • No one asked him any more questions that day • *A dying man needs your help*, said the unfamiliar voice on the phone • Subway stations—and this astonished me—do not remain open all night • Those horrible dead trees burnt charcoal black • Her bones were filled with tree spirits • They looked to me, as though I had the answers • Home turned out to be a cave of ice, which she found by getting lost in winter woods • The cop handed me the gun and I aimed it at my attacker and looked into his eyes • One smooth pebble, ground by the action of a glacier • Surely we are prepared to make contact • It was good bread • As always • The drums were a comfort • But perfection brings its own pain • The heat helped • And feathers *still* seem like little pieces of horror dropped into our world • The half that didn't die looked on with bewilderment and a kind of hope • I put the worm on the hook • They each grabbed onto a rope and did their best to crawl out of the pit • His only regret, as he waited for the pop, was that he couldn't be there • We guessed as much • He gave me pottery for our fourth anniversary, but I didn't care • The soaring exultant color of blue • She sees the truth, always • We shared the night like it had been concocted just for us • No more • We didn't marry, but we did raise children, lots of them, and every one went on to take a spouse • Listen, it's just a story, nothing to get upset over, not really • Then the school bell called us in from the horror • I landed in Seattle just in time to catch an Uber to the service • But that was the problem • No more tall tales, okay? • But that was a long time ago, another era, really • Paris will always have us • Smoke season came and killed everyone's spirit • Raindrops spattered against the windshield until I turned on the wipers and they commenced chattering over the glass, smearing the water and rendering my view even worse than I had imagined it could be • But it never lasts more than a day or two • I agreed • She wanted answers, but I had none for her that would satisfy truth and her heart • Like many artists, she had her own view of things • The street sign floated past us • "No other way possible," she said • When every breath feels like your last, I found it was easy to be kind • No one's fault, except, maybe, Glen's • I decided it was going to be all right • Mouse parts littered the floor •

"Just beautiful" • I wet my thumb and forefinger on my tongue and pressed both digits against the wick, snuffing out the flame • She had conquered one world and was ready to tackle her own • No need for anyone to make their suicide messy and nightmare-inducing, not when there are good clean alternatives • I would have preferred a living breathing nightmare to the story he told that night • I followed her • We raised anchor and set sail without a moment's regret • The sun was the wrong color, everyone agreed • You could say he was the weak silent type • All languages take something from you that you don't want to let go • Nothing left but hope, and that's never enough • No one understood the house was not built by Darcy • He tried to make the minute last an hour • The kraken's body slipped into the water, a blurry mass, than disappeared from view • I tapped the pipe on the ashtray and out came a dusting of ash along with several tiny insects that skittered around in circles • A sharp biting pain in my elbow • A disappointment, to be sure • His way, always • My nation's wound became my wound • Janice and his shadow held him close to the earth • No one will ever know, or want to know • The doctor was right • The bears were hungry and numerous • The thundercloud was wet and warm and I pulled it down to the ground and reveled in its wild frenzy, soaking me with water and so much love • His fingers were still trembling, but there was a smile on his lips as he dialed Eileen's number • Judgement doesn't happen in a day • The constable should have kept out of the matter and that is all I have to say on the subject • That's how I saw it, anyway • Too many corpses for one life to have to witness • The train whistle faded and died under the clatter of the wheels on the track • Nothing but sadness • The papery texture of life will keep you strong and whole • My hair was perfect • The future was done • I suppose that's why people call it punishment • Everyone knows games are a waste of time and talent • We destroyed the time machine and turned from the rubble we produced to face life in the wilds of the Pleistocene • But then, my second marriage was less love story and more short conversation • I filled the pool with acid • She led him to the spot where I had last been seen • The missing dogs • They kept up the fakery with admirable energy • It won't happen again • A dark train determined to stay on track • His ship, his rules • You should never worry about injustice • I never missed a single one of my superpowers • I covered my face against their stares, knowing that a crying old man just makes people embarrassed and sad • You could view it as a limit to belief • She called down the Furies and destroyed the dollhouse • Wasn't that the way civilized people behaved? • Long enough for the retinas to burn out and for darkness—so welcome, so shaded, so familiar—to return and bring me all the comfort I could stand • Especially if you believe time is an illusion • The house had tears of its own • No reason to expect anything more • The only thing I know for sure is that all I have related here is true to the best of my knowledge and memory • I tossed the thumb drive overboard • We hitched up the trailer and headed north • The house, it turned out, spoke Spanish • "You need to learn to always look for a better way," she said • No one had to be there • Be careful what you abhor • Tape across my heart • We named her Cassandra • Sometimes it just takes a while to notice the obvious • Yeah, okay • You would have a hard time spelling it anyway • So much refusal from so many • His song was not music to anyone's ears, no matter what the critics said • I prayed they were all dead and I was alone • It was, as Ashley predicted, an unholy mess • Don't live in the past • Seedless grapes • But the mechanics of death, once in place, ground on much too slowly for me and for Myra, who died three weeks later, strongly against her wish to go quickly and quietly • We then settled in for a long cold winter • The ships crawled along the horizon until they were lost in the fog • I didn't feel like a win-ner • So many rats • I dreamed that Mom got that stupid flag, and I dreamed that Chandra knew she had done the right thing • They had strange appetites, all of them • But I had solved my first murder and knew I would go on doing so until I drew my last breath • How do I do it without losing face? • I finally understood what she meant • The rails, supported by wooden ties, receded to infinity in front of me • But all the shooting, all the blood, it turned me from a civilized being to a savage beast, and I never turned back • I did not see the point, then or ever • No one in my group remembered why • The card turned out to be the hanged man • I called it my best • He called me old • But the Cascades, solitary sentinels, lived long in my heart • I couldn't turn it off • The deposition was a trivial thing • The thing is, *my* mannequins didn't scream • On the edge of the orchard • I said thank you, which was something she did not want to hear as she fell upon me, fists pummeling and feet kicking • Never give up smoking if you know what's good for you • It is time to mourn • You could say the land kidnapped me • But she had street smarts and I didn't • The shuttle was dead • But I could not have known any of that • Leaving the hospital was like entering a prison • One of the great lies is that violence solves nothing • I returned to sit with her on the edge of the couch • Never expected to get accolades for my actions • Life has only one imperative • Salem was our paradise • It is always best to delete your own account • Well, sure, we all have treachery in our hearts • He was working up some sass to throw at his mother, but he was stopped before he could get into it by her hand across his face, turning the whole world red and blurry and wrong • That was the set up • The walk home was the most pleasant he had ever had • The penultimate crime • I suppose you could call it an escape, of sorts • The difference was neither enlightening nor entertaining • It was clothing optional, after all • It wasn't my fault, I'm pretty sure • Vanished • Joanna was • I blinked, turning off my sensors, and lived in the welcome silence for an indeterminate length of time • I stare at the image in the mirror and pray for amnesia • Night found us, which was a fate no one should endure • And decided that dining from dumpsters was not the worst thing that could happen to a person • Not in Saskatoon, anyway • No, I mean it, endings are really really hard • But icebergs, like stories, hide much of their substance beneath the surface

About the Author

Mario Milosevic's books include include *Labor Days, Terrastina and Mazolli, Animal Life, The Last Giant,* and *The Coma Monologues.* He lives in the desert Southwest of the United States. mariowrites.com.